MERMAIDS' TALES

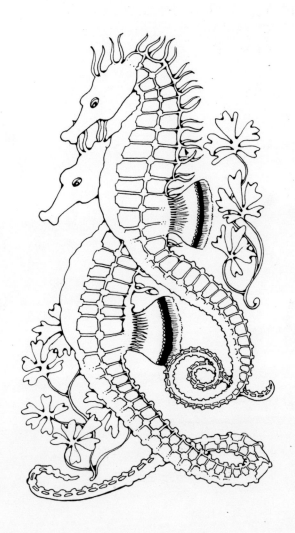

By the same author

MR JUMBLE'S TOY SHOP
THREE'S COMPANY
THE NOAH'S ARK

and other titles

MERMAIDS' TALES

RUTH AINSWORTH

With line drawings by
Dandi Palmer

LUTTERWORTH PRESS · GUILDFORD AND LONDON

CONTENTS

Chapter 1

LESSONS UNDER THE SEA

'WHY MUST I learn to play the harp?' asked Laver crossly. She was a little mermaid with long golden hair and a green fishy tail, and she sat on a rock at the bottom of the sea, twanging a small golden harp.

Her mother sat on a larger rock, giving her little daughter her harp lesson, guiding the thin greenish fingers with patience that never ran out.

'All mermaids have to learn to play the harp,' she said softly. 'Every single one.'

'But why, why, why?' asked Laver, shaking her harp angrily.

'You will find it very useful. You can charm sea-monsters when you happen to meet them, so that they lie at ease, blissfully listening. If they were not under the spell of the music, they might decide to crunch you for their dinner. Sea-monsters are often very large and very hungry.'

'That might be useful,' said Laver, who had never, yet, seen a sea-monster. She was not allowed to explore very far on her own and was content to make friends with the fishes and crabs and lobsters, and other small creatures.

'Then there are human beings you can charm, particularly sailors. Think how useful Billy Bones is to us. He's so good with the little ones that I don't think I

7

could manage without him. When he heard my harp music, he left his ship *The Rising Star*, and came to live with us. That was years ago, when you were a tiny baby in a cradle.'

Laver picked up her harp with a sigh. Still, it would be rather useful to charm hungry sea-monsters, and perhaps sailors too, if they were as kind as Billy Bones.

While Laver was playing her harp, her father swam by, gleaming and powerful. He was one of the Lords of the Sea and wore a crown round his forehead. He stroked her hair lightly with the finger on which he wore a golden ring.

'Well done, my little daughter. Practise well and you may one day be as good a harpist as your mother.'

Laver decided, there and then, that she would practise, and she played a piece three times over to show she really meant it.

While she was playing, her elder sister, Emerald, was combing her long fair hair with a comb made from a narwhal's tusk. Mermaids have to keep their hair without a knot or tangle in it, and this takes time. When they are very young, their mothers do it for them—or in this family, Billy Bones the sailor, who was gentle and patient with the comb—but Emerald and Laver were now thought old enough to do their own hair.

'I wish I wasn't old enough to comb my own hair,' said Emerald, chucking roughly at the comb. 'Billy, won't you give me a hand? It's full of tangles this morning and the more I comb, the worse it gets.'

'Your mother says I'm to leave you to it,' said Billy,

*'A fine, upstanding lad like you needs to know a knot
or two,' Billy Bones told Bubbles.*

'and I wouldn't disobey that sweet lady for the world.
Anyhow, I'm busy giving your brother Bubbles a lesson
in knot-tying.'

Bubbles was a little merman, with a head of curls like
his father. All the mermen, large and small, had short
curls, while all the mermaids had long straight hair. It
grew that way.

'How stupid to learn to tie knots when I'm spending
hours trying to untangle them,' said Emerald.

'That's what I think,' agreed Bubbles.

'Now, now,' said Billy Bones. 'None of that nonsense. A fine, upstanding lad like you needs to know a knot or two, safe and reliable and quick. A knot that neither wind nor water can loosen, may save a man's life. Now show me a clove-hitch and a running bowline, and then that'll do for today. Remember—left over right and pull it tight.'

Bubbles did his best with the length of rope and when Billy Bones was satisfied, he darted away with a flick of his silver tail. Just then the harp lesson came to an end, as well, and Emerald drew the comb through the very last tangle.

So the three sea-children frisked and frolicked in their freedom.

Chapter 2

THE WRECK

THOUGH THE SEA-CHILDREN lived in the sea, they were not, yet, allowed to go wherever they liked. The cave where they lived was surrounded, on all sides, by seaweed with a purple tinge to it.

'Stay in the purple patch,' said their mother. 'When you go further your father or I must be with you. There's lots of room in the purple patch for you to play your games.'

'Why?' said Bubbles.

'Why?' said Emerald.

'Why?' said Laver.

'Because there are dangers beyond the purple patch. When you are older, you'll know what to do, but till then, it's not safe.'

'Sea-monsters?' asked Laver.

'Perhaps. And you know what a hungry sea-monster can do. Sea-children make a tender morsel.'

The children were usually content with their purple patch, but today Bubbles had something secret to show them.

'Follow me,' he said, darting away so fast that his sisters could only just keep his curly head and silvery tail in sight. But they were used to playing follow-my-leader and the fact that they did not know where he was leading them made them feel excited. They were nearly out of the purple patch and the seaweed was mostly pink and green, when Bubbles stopped and the girls caught up with him.

'Look,' he said. 'What do you think it is?'

The children would have had no idea if Billy Bones had not been such a wonderful story-teller.

'It must be a wreck,' said Laver, looking at the large, dark object which rested on the bed of the ocean, leaning to one side.

'Yes, a real wreck,' said Bubbles. 'The wreck of a ship that sank.'

'Can we get inside?'

'Why not? This cabin window is just a hole. I'll go first.'

Quietly and carefully they swam through the nearest window and soon felt brave enough to look everywhere. Most of the things they saw were strange to them, but they recognised beds and curtains and cups. These they had themselves in their rocky cave. In one cabin there were small objects shaped rather like themselves, but with legs like Billy Bones instead of tails.

'They're dolls,' said Emerald, picking one up. 'Billy says that sad poem about a doll sometimes, you know the one that begins *I once had a sweet little doll, dears.*"

'I know,' said Laver, 'and she lost it.'

'Well, I shan't lose mine, I'll take great care of her,' said Emerald, cradling one of the dolls tenderly.

'I'll have this one. It's a doll baby, I think.' Laver took the baby in her arms.

'They're dolls,' said Emerald, *picking one up.*

'I'll have this one,' said Bubbles, 'dressed like Billy Bones. It's a sailor doll.'

They were very pleased with their new dolls and began to make up games with them. Then they played hide-and-seek and they forgot all about time.

'We must go,' said Bubbles. 'But we can come back.'

'Let's explore a little more,' said Emerald, 'then we'll go. What's in this room? It's dark—' She hesitated. 'Come with me.'

They all crowded in and the door closed behind them with a sharp click.

'I don't like it. I keep bumping into things,' wailed Laver.

'I can't breathe properly.'

'Get your hair out of my face!'

'I don't know where your face *is*.'

'Open the door. Who's nearest?'

'I am. But it hasn't a handle.'

They felt over every inch of the door but found no way of opening it.

'We're prisoners.'

'No one knows we are here, so no one can rescue us.'

'We shall starve.'

They all cried and cried because they had never been so frightened before.

'I've found a rope dangling down,' said Bubbles. 'I'll give it a pull. You never know. Something might happen.'

He pulled with all his strength and they heard a deep, echoing boom! boom! boom!

'Someone may hear and look for us,' said Emerald. 'Let me have a go.'

They pulled in turn and they pulled all together.

Away in the purple patch, Billy Bones stopped polishing an amber lamp and said:

'I know that sound. It's a ship's bell. Someone may be in distress.'

'Where are the older children?' said the Mermaid Mother. No one had seen them since Laver's harp lesson.

'I'll find them,' said Billy Bones, whose life under the sea had taught him to swim almost as well as a merman.

He made off, guided by the boom of the bell, the Mermaid Mother close behind. The sound led them to the wreck, and Billy Bones, who knew his way about a ship, soon found where the children were imprisoned.

'You need a special key to get out from the inside,' he said, opening the door.

The children got over their fright first and soon went back to playing with their dolls, though they did not look forward to the scolding their father, the Lord of the Sea, would give them when he came home.

But their mother was pale and cold with shock and Billy Bones made her some seaweed tea in the best pearly teapot.

'Children will be children the world over,' he said as he poured her a cup. 'They mean no harm.'

Chapter 3

THE BEACH

THE CHILDREN NEVER got tired of asking 'When shall we be old enough to do this? To do that? To do something else?' They were taken by surprise when suddenly their mother said:

'Now you three are old enough to come with me to the beach at low tide. You will see many wonderful sights. There may be human children, walking on two legs, and playing on the sand and in the shallow pools.'

'No tails?' said Laver.

'Never a tail among them. And on their heads hair of many colours, black and brown and even red. And some with golden hair like yours.'

'I want to see someone with red hair,' said Emerald.

'You may be lucky,' said their mother. 'But you must do exactly what I say. There are always dangers when children of the sea meet with children of the land.'

'What kind of dangers?' asked Bubbles.

Their mother hesitated. 'Human children like to collect things and take them away. They like chasing things. There's no telling, but they might want to capture a sea-child and keep it.'

'They won't catch *me!*' said Bubbles. 'I'd bite.'

'And I'd do two turns and a twist and slip away,' said Laver.

'It's safest to keep out of reach,' said Emerald.

'That's what we'll all do,' agreed her mother.

When the tide was going out, they swam towards Sandy Bay. Past the wreck: through waving seaweed of many colours: and then the water grew warmer and lighter, and rocks appeared.

'We'll stay close to this rock covered with seaweed, as it will give us good cover. Keep under water except for your faces, and spy through the seaweed. Watch and keep still,' said their mother.

At first the sea-children found the sun so dazzling after the cloudy deep where they lived that they could see very little. Gradually they became used to the brightness and could separate the blue sky from the yellow sand and the shimmering sea. Then they saw the human children, big and small, playing on the sand and in the shallow pools.

Some were making sand castles, or sand pies. Some were poking around in the pools and catching shrimps and tiny crabs to put in their buckets. Each was busy and happy, and one, as Laver quickly pointed out, had red hair.

'Is this the beach where Billy Bones played when he was a little boy?' asked Bubbles. 'He had a wooden spade and a red bucket and a shrimping net. He told us so.'

'Very like this, I expect. Keep your voices down.'

The sea-children could have watched for ever. They specially liked the other children's feet and toes.

'They don't swim very well,' said Emerald. 'They

17

splash and puff. Our little ones at home do better, even the baby.'

'But they run well,' said Laver. 'Our baby can't even stand though she can swim a little. I wish I had a coloured ball like the one those children are throwing and catching.'

A fishing boat landed and the crew of big, burly fishermen leapt out in their blue jerseys and began spreading their nets to dry in the sun.

'Some are just boys like me,' said Bubbles.

'They are learning to be fishermen like their fathers,' said his mother. 'But come—it's time to go home. We won't stay and watch the fishermen. It's too sad a sight. Their boat is full of beautiful gleaming fish they have caught in their nets. All dead. Never to swim again. And there are stories—I fear true ones—of mermaids who were caught in the nets.'

'What happened to them?' whispered Laver.

'They were never seen again in the kingdom of the sea. Never again. Now come, the little ones at home will be missing me.'

'They've got Billy Bones. Stay a few minutes longer!' begged the children.

'No. The fishing boat has spoiled the day for me. We have stayed too long.'

When they were back in their rocky cave, the sea-children could not stop talking. They had seen sights of which they had only heard in Billy Bones' stories. They had seen another world, the world of dry land where mortals led their mysterious lives.

They told Billy Bones about the fishing boat and the
nets and their mother's fear and sadness.

'She has cause to feel sorrow, that sweet lady,'
said Billy Bones. 'Before you three were born, she gave
birth to a son—a great wanderer though he was little
more than a baby. And he got caught in a net. She can
hardly bear the sight of a fishing boat since, and small
wonder.'

After this first sight of the beach and the land-children,
the sea-children begged every day to swim shoreward
when the tide was low. Their mother was fearful, but
their father, the Lord of the Sea, thought differently.

'You'll come to no harm if you are obedient and
sensible,' he said. 'Stay by the rock, where your mother
took you. It is called Table Rock. Raise only your
heads above the water and if a swimmer should
approach, dive instantly and make for home.'

'And don't go near a fisherman or his nets, or a
boat,' added their mother.

The children promised and there began a delightful
series of visits to the beach, filled with wonder and
mystery. Every day they saw something new and came
back with another tale to tell Billy Bones or whoever
would listen.

Laver watched the little girl with red hair. She often
played alone, making gardens in the sand, decorating
them with shells and seaweed and pebbles. She made
low walls of sand and picked twigs of tamarisk which
grew on the cliffs, to make trees and shady places. Laver
was always the last to make for home because she went

as close as she dared to the little gardens to see exactly how the shells and pebbles were arranged.

Once the sea-children visited the beach in the middle of the night. There was not a child in sight. The land-children were all asleep in bed, just as Emerald, Bubbles and Laver should have been themselves—and would have been if watchful Billy Bones hadn't been busy with one of the little ones, who had toothache and couldn't go to sleep. While he was soothing the baby, the older children slipped out of the cave.

'Let's go to the beach, it's quite safe,' suggested Bubbles.

There they wandered among the sand pies and castles and gardens, soon to be swept away as the tide was coming in fast.

'Look!' said Emerald. 'Look what I've found! A child has left his spade stuck in a castle for a flagstaff. There's a seaweed flag fastened to it. Let's take it home.'

'Isn't it stealing?' said Laver.

'Of course not. The sea's green fingers will snatch it away soon enough and toss it among the waves. It will have drifted miles away by morning. It's more good to us than to the sea who has more treasures than he can count. What do you think, Bubbles?'

'The child who owns the spade will never see it again, that's certain. We may just as well have it, Emerald is quite right,' said Bubbles.

The beach was so pleasant in the soft, silvery light that the three did not want to leave, but they were afraid they might be missed. So they reluctantly turned away and swam home, Emerald holding her new spade.

They all crept into their pearly bed and drew the seaweed curtains round them and fell asleep. So Billy Bones found them when the crying baby had dropped off at last. He wondered a little at the wooden spade Emerald had beside her, on her pillow, but he was never one to ask unnecessary questions or tell tales.

The spade came in very useful and Billy made them two more from loose timbers from the wreck. Then the children could make castles and forts out of the sand at the bottom of the sea.

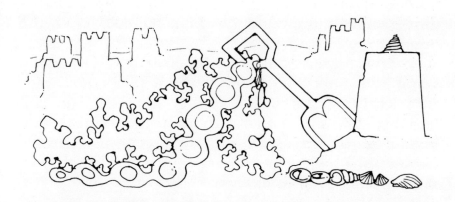

Chapter 4

SUNBURN

LIFE WAS VERY different now that Emerald and Laver and Bubbles were considered sensible enough to amuse themselves and go further afield, if they were careful to remember the way back. They had certain duties to perform each day before they were free to please themselves. The girls had their harp lessons, and their long golden hair to comb. Bubbles had his knots to practise, and all three had to learn the names of the countless creatures who lived in the sea, the fishes and seaweeds and crabs and shrimps and shells, which some-times seemed more numerous than the pebbles on the beach.

'Learn a few every day,' said their father. 'Gradually you'll add more and more. Never bother your heads with learning *all* about anything. I, myself, am still learning, that's all you can hope to do. I hear that human beings are just the same. I have seen venerable old men with white beards reading books. They, too, are learning, even in old age.'

When their tasks were done and their lessons learned, tested afterwards by their mother or Billy Bones, they were free. Off they went, with flickering tails and eager faces, often to Sandy Bay, if the tide were right.

Laver was fascinated by the brown tan on the land-children's arms and legs and bodies. She noticed how white they were when they first came to the seaside, and how brown they were when their holidays ended. Their fathers and mothers often lay in the sun all day, sometimes on their fronts, and sometimes on their backs. She described this habit to her mother.

'Strange are the ways of land-people,' said her mother. 'They have this odd wish to turn their white skins brown by lying in the sun. I think they look much more becoming white, but they think otherwise. It is a harmless occupation. Perhaps the sun does them good in ways we do not understand. How much prettier you look, my darlings,' and she gazed with love and admiration at her three older children, and the pale greenish tinge of their skins.

Laver was not convinced that she *did* look prettier. She took to swimming to Table Rock, when the other two were playing elsewhere, and she daringly climbed on to the top and lay there, with the sun pouring its golden warmth all over her, if the tide were low enough.

At first it dazzled her eyes, so she kept them shut and just let herself dream in a drowsy way. Time slipped by without her noticing. Sometimes she dozed until the sun set below the horizon and the sudden chill woke her up.

Once she opened her eyes to see the face of a man, a swimmer, level with her own. He had a black beard and dark eyes and bushy eyebrows. The surprise on her face was not as great as the amazement—almost horror—on his. He turned his head and called to some companions:

'Come quickly! A mermaid! It's unbelievable!'

23

'Come quickly! A mermaid! It's unbelievable!'

These few seconds brought Laver to her senses and she slipped under the water and made for home, too rapidly to hear the men arguing together.

'Mermaid my foot! You're out of your mind!'

'But I tell you she was lying there asleep, golden hair and fishy tail and all.'

'Then where is she now?'

'Gone down to the bottom of the sea, I suppose. But look here. Isn't this proof?'

He picked a long, golden hair from among the tangled seaweed. 'Mermaid's hair.'

His friends examined it in turn. It certainly looked like hair. But one hair was not enough to convince them.

'You were suffering from a touch of sun, old chap. You're seeing things. I shouldn't tell anyone, if I were you. They might think you were off your head. You just keep quiet and go to bed early.'

'And buy a sunhat,' suggested someone else.

They swam lazily to shore. The first swimmer kept the golden hair in his pocket notebook for years. It reminded him of one of the most wonderful experiences of his life, the day when he had seen a little mermaid sleeping on a seaweedy rock. The only person who ever believed him was his little daughter Alice who could always be settled for sleep if told the story of how Daddy saw a mermaid. He showed her the golden hair, too, safe in his notebook, but she would have believed the story without any proof.

Though Laver liked the warmth of the sun, it did not really agree with her. The scales on her tail began to lose their beautiful sheen and her skin looked less clear and transparent, even a little blotchy. Her mother looked at her anxiously and called her husband, the Lord of the Sea, to consider the change in his daughter's appearance.

'Scales certainly dull,' he pronounced. 'And skin not in a healthy state. Give her a daily dose of Tonic of Salt. And beware of direct sunlight,' he added. 'It is not meant for sea-people. We flourish in the soft, shadowy depths of the ocean where we are born.'

But as Laver felt perfectly well, and had become very

fond of her sunbathing on the rock, she did not give it up entirely. Perhaps the blotches on her arms meant that they were about to turn to the warm brown she so much admired, and desired. So she neglected her father's warning and made up her mind to sunbathe just once more. Only once more, she said to herself, and then never again. Surely that would not be very naughty?

The next day was particularly sunny and low tide came in the afternoon. Emerald and Bubbles were hunting for sea-snails to put in a little rocky hollow they had made. The sea-snails kept escaping and the children had to invent new ways of keeping them confined.

When Laver arrived at Table Rock there were many human children playing on the beach and once more she admired their warm, brown skins. There were no swimmers in sight, or fishing boats, and she closed her eyes and lay on the cool seaweedy rock. The sunshine poured all over her; sometimes she turned over to let it reach another part of her, the back of her neck and her shoulders. Soon she fell asleep.

Chapter 5

ONCE TOO OFTEN

T HE TIDE REACHED its lowest point and then turned and began to come in. The children left the beach to go home for their suppers, begging in vain for just five minutes more. The water crept up the sides of Table Rock and began to swirl over the top. This would have wakened a land-child at once, but mermaids are used to sleeping in the water. Laver never stirred. The breaking of the waves over her lulled her into a deeper sleep.

The beach was now empty and the tide was swallowing up all the work that had taken the children half the day. Their footprints in the sand went first. Then the little ones' sand pies. Then the castles, even a massive one that some big children had made, helped in the end by several fathers. They had strengthened the walls with stones, but these were nothing to the might of the sea. All disappeared under the foaming waves with the shells and seaweed that the children had added for decoration.

Then, noticed only by the swooping gulls, a small fishing boat appeared far out to sea, first a mere speck, then getting nearer and clearer. There were two men and a boy inside, all with sunburned faces, and all wearing navy jersies.

'Careful, Davy lad,' called one of the men. 'You're steering us mighty near Table Rock.'

'But look what's *on* Table Rock!' called the other. 'Go carefully, Davy. There's a mermaid asleep there.'

They shipped their oars and let the boat drift near.

'Shall I lean out and catch hold of her?' asked the boy Davy, his eyes shining.

'I've heard tales that they are slippery as fish,' said his father. 'You'd not be able to hold her.'

'We can throw the net over her,' said the other man, Peter. 'Then we can gather her up safely. Steady there, and I'll cast it.'

He stood up, net in hand, and flung it towards the rock. The first time it fell short and flopped back into the water, but the second time it landed, fair and square, over the sleeping Laver. As the rough net touched her, she sat up in terror. Was it a nightmare, this boat, the three fishermen, and the clinging, clutching net?

She tried to turn and twist and slip away, but she was hampered on every side. She was held fast. A prisoner, like one of the silver fish that met their end in a fisherman's net.

Peter, and Davy's father, whose name was Patrick, lifted her gently into their boat and rowed to shore. She was too frightened to realise what was happening. She was carried up the beach and into the little white-washed hut where Patrick and Davy lived. They unwound the net and at once she darted for the door. Round and round the little room she bounded, evading hands that tried to hold her, and knocking painfully into the chairs and the table.

When she was tired out, she sank down on to the floor. Patrick took her on his lap, hushing her and rocking her. Through her fear, she felt his kindness and gentleness.

'Don't take on so, my pretty. Nothing can harm you here. There's nothing to fear. It's different, I know, from where you came, lass, but you'll soon get accustomed to our ways. I live here with Davy, my son, all on our own because my wife died some years ago.'

When she stopped shivering and crying, Davy brought a length of thin green cord and Patrick tied it round her waist, first putting it over her shoulders like a harness. He tied the free end to a hook in the wall.

'It's soft and won't hurt you, but we can't risk losing you now we've found you. Look, you can move freely around the place and fetch anything you want and do what you like.' Patrick tied the last knot.

Davy had been silent. Now he took her cold greenish hand in his and knelt on the rug beside her.

'And you can play. You're only a little girl. We'll play together. I'll teach you my games and you must teach me yours. We'll have fun—I've always wanted a sister. What shall we call you?'

'Laver is my name.'

'That's a pretty name, lass, and not known in these parts,' said Patrick.

'It is the name of a seaweed.'

Laver refused all they offered her for supper but drank a mug of milk. The cottage was tiny, only the living-room and the bedroom where Davy and his father slept. But they made her a bed on the sofa and covered her with a blanket.

'Too hot,' she whispered, so in its place they put a green silk counterpane, unfolded from tissue paper in a drawer. She knew it was a household treasure, fringed and patterned with gold.

'Silk,' said Davy. 'Real silk.'

'Now try to sleep, Laver. You're worn out with all your new experiences. Tomorrow you'll feel better.'

I'll never sleep a wink, not ever, she thought, but as she was thinking this, sleep overcame her. She never heard Patrick and Davy tip-toeing about the room or saw the soft glow of the lamp, or felt gentle hands stroking her hair. She lay all night in a long, dreamless sleep, deep and peaceful as the ocean from whence she had come.

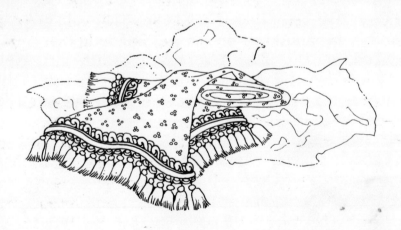

Chapter 6

THE FISHERMAN'S HUT

WHEN LAVER WOKE up, the morning sun was streaming into the hut. Patrick and Davy were having their breakfast and she accepted another mug of milk and a few fingers of brown bread and honey. They were handed to her on a china plate painted with flowers and butterflies. Homesick though she was, she knew these strange people were kind and bringing out their few precious possessions to please her. She looked intently at the plate and said, 'Pretty.'

Davy looked pleased.

'I must be off to work with Peter,' said Patrick, 'but as this is your first day, Davy will stay and take care of you. Remember what I told you, Davy, admit no one, friend or stranger. And you remember the other thing?'

'Yes, Father.'

Patrick had hardly closed the hut door before Laver turned to Davy and begged him to set her free.

'Please, please, please, I'll bring you treasures from the sea as a reward. Pearl and amber and coral.'

'I don't want a reward for giving you pleasure. I'd do anything in the world for you, except disobey my father. He has been both father and mother to me since my mother died. He's a good man.'

'I know,' said Laver sadly. 'I feel he is.'

Laver looked intently at the plate.

'Would you disobey your father?'

Laver thought of the Lord of the Sea, crowned and majestic, but loving.

'I did disobey him once. He told me not to sunbathe

32

again and I did, on Table Rock. Just once more, I said to myself. Just once more. And see where it has brought me.'

The tears brimmed her eyes.

Davy took her hand.

'You'll get used to living with us,' he said. 'It'll just take time. Now help me to dry the dishes.'

As Davy washed the bowls and plates and spoons, Laver soon learned how to dry them. Then Davy scrubbed some potatoes for supper and cooked some apples. Next they had a game of marbles.

Laver forgot to be miserable and laughed out loud as she won three marbles for herself. Davy gave her an old purse to keep them in.

He also washed his comb, which was old with some teeth missing, but clean as a new pin when he offered it to her. Laver combed her long golden hair and Davy helped with one or two tangles.

For some weeks Laver lived with the fisherfolk. Patrick and Davy were delighted when they found she could thread a needle and sew. She mended holes in their socks and sewed on missing buttons. They themselves were not handy with a needle, though they did their best.

Sometimes Davy had to go out with his father, and then the hut door was locked. When Laver heard the key turn in the lock, she did not feel frightened at the thought of being left by herself. She took out the sewing basket or did something to surprise them. Once she washed the china dogs that stood on the mantelpiece, and she embroidered *P* and *D* in the corner of Patrick's and Davy's best handkerchiefs.

What she liked best of all was being read to. Billy Bones had told the sea-children a few stories and poems that he remembered, but Davy had real books, with coloured pictures, and he was never tired of reading her favourites over and over again. She liked *Hansel and Gretel* best, and *Beauty and the Beast*.

Davy promised he would teach her to read and she had a reading lesson every day. There seemed a great deal to remember, but she learned to write her name with no mistakes. She could write *DAVY* too. Her favourite letter was *V* because it was easy, and both she and Davy had it in their names.

One evening when the beach was deserted and the moon had risen, Patrick said to her:

'How would you like to go for a swim? It's a fine night.'

Davy came too, and they boarded the little boat and launched it. After rowing well away from the shore, Patrick helped Laver over the side into the shimmering water, holding fast to the end of the green cord.

The feel of the salt water, and the smell of it, gave Laver a deep desire for freedom and she fought and struggled with her harness like a wild thing. She bit and tore at the knots, diving as deeply as the tether would allow. But the harness never yielded. The knots were safe, sure fisherman's knots, as reliable as Billy Bones' sailor's knots. Then, exhausted, she let herself float gently along beside the boat, with an occasional flap of her tail or her thin green arms.

'That's my good maiden,' said Patrick, and Davy slipped into the water beside her, swimming with her, sometimes holding on to the boat with one hand and holding Laver's hand with the other. Gradually her mood changed. She felt peaceful, almost happy, and Davy seemed like a brother. Whenever she turned her head and looked at him, he smiled back and she smiled too, while up above them, in the boat, good patient Patrick kept watch over them.

Chapter 7

TAP, TAP ON THE WINDOW

LIFE WAS STILL strange for Laver, and different for Patrick and Davy in other ways. The fisherfolk in the village could not understand why they were no longer welcome in the white-washed hut, for a chat or a cup of tea.

Patrick bought a doll for Laver and she spent hours, when alone, making clothes for it and playing with it. It was far prettier than the doll she found in the wreck.

Patrick and Davy saw no reason why things should not go on like this for ever. In time, they might even allow their friends to meet Laver. It was much more comfortable finding their buttons sewn on and their supper ready when they came back after fishing, and for Davy to have a sister and Patrick a daughter.

As for Laver, the ceaseless sound of waves breaking no longer made her weep, and when she suddenly felt homesick she played with her doll or worked at her lessons. But the homesickness never left her. Memories of her mermaid days came crowding in upon her, with the scents and sounds and magic of the sea, and often she felt she could not bear the dry air of the cottage and the harness that constricted her.

Then nothing but a moonlight swim would calm and comfort her.

One night Laver heard a tapping on the window pane, tap-tap-tap. She slid off her couch and went towards the window. It was dark, but she could just make out Bubbles' face, pressed against the glass, and his fair curls. He signed to her to open the window wider. This she did, flinching at every crack and creak.

'Bubbles!' she whispered. 'How did you get here?'

'Never mind how. That can wait. It's how *you* can get back home to us. I have brought help. Here is your harp.'

'My harp? I've almost forgotten how to play it.'

'Of course you haven't. No mermaid forgets how to play her harp, it would be like forgetting how to swim. You must charm these horrid fisher-people with your harp and then they'll have to let you go. Think how Mother charmed Billy Bones to leave his ship and his shipmates and throw in his lot with us sea-people.'

'But they aren't horrid fisher-people,' said Laver. 'They're kind and gentle and are always trying to please me. Davy is like a brother—almost,' she added, seeing the disappointment on Bubbles' face.

'You love him better than me,' muttered Bubbles.

'I don't—oh, I can't explain. It's so different. But I do love him, and I love Patrick too.'

'Think of us, your real family,' begged Bubbles. 'Mother weeps day and night. The little ones are off their food. Emerald sits and mopes most of the day in the shadow of a rock. I never have any fun and I get nightmares that the fisher-people have sliced you up and fried you in a pan.'

The last remark made Laver smile.

'They'd as soon slice each other up as harm one of my scales or a hair of my head.'

'But you'll do it—you'll charm them?'

'Yes, I'll do it; give me my harp, and thank you, Bubbles.'

'Here is your harp,' said Bubbles.

She looked round for somewhere to hide her harp. The hut was so small that there were few hiding-places to choose from. In the end, she slipped it inside the cushion that served her as a pillow. During the day, this cushion was put away in a cupboard. As she handled her golden harp she longed to pluck the strings.

She hoped she could remember the charm music. It

38

was rather difficult. She hummed it softly to herself. Yes, she remembered the tune. Her mother had told her that it was the most beautiful and powerful music in the world.

Chapter 8

THE LAST DAY

THAT DAY PATRICK did not need Davy's help with the boat and he was left at home. This was usually a treat for Laver but, for the first time, she was sorry. Had she been left alone, she could have practised on her harp.

As it was, Davy was especially kind and thoughtful. He undid the tangles in her hair with gentle fingers and read her favourite stories. Her reading lesson went well and she read 'The sand is yellow and the sea is green' all by herself. Then they played games and Davy made her a little boat out of a walnut shell and a ring of dancing people out of paper. Laver had never loved him more or felt more like his real sister. Every time she remembered the harp in the cupboard, hidden inside the cushion, she sighed.

'You're not happy today,' said Davy. 'You have secret thoughts that make you sigh. Tell me what's wrong. I can keep a secret. Brothers and sisters can tell each other anything.'

He looked at her so appealingly that tears brimmed her eyes and rolled down her pale cheeks. Davy wiped them away with his best handkerchief, the one with *D* embroidered in the corner.

'I can't,' he heard her murmur, 'I wish I could, but I can't.'

'Then I won't ask you again. It's time we set the table for supper. I'll slip out for a few sea-pinks, I know you like flowers on the table.'

He was soon back and Laver arranged the pinks in a cracked cup (there were no vases in the hut).

Patrick was home late, hungry and tired. Laver guessed he had had a heavy catch. But he had never talked about his day's fishing since he discovered how it distressed Laver to hear of the many silvery fish that would never swim again.

So he and Davy went early to bed, and Laver did the same.

'No, let me do it,' she called sharply to Davy when he went to the cupboard to get her pillow. 'I know just how I like it.'

He looked hurt at being spoken to so crossly, but said nothing in return.

'You're tired too, by the sound of it,' said Patrick, kissing her goodnight. 'We shall all feel better in the morning,' and he tucked the silken quilt lightly over her.

It was all Laver could do not to throw her arms round his neck and hug him closely, this strange land-being who had become an important part of her life.

Laver lay awake long after Patrick and Davy had fallen asleep. She could hear their deep, even breathing through the wall. Then, when she had gathered all her courage together, she slipped off the couch, took the golden harp in her hands and opened the door into the bedroom. She began to play.

41

The cottage was filled with the haunting, magical music.

Soon the cottage was filled with the haunting, magical music of the charm. Patrick and Davy got out of their beds and walked slowly into the living room. Their eyes were open, but they looked as if they were sleep-walking. There was no expression on their faces. Just the blankness of deep sleep. Laver played on, trying to hide the trembling of her hands.

'Take off my harness, please, Patrick.'

Patrick showed no surprise. He undid the knots, one

42

by one, even the last tight secret one that only he could tie.

'Go back to your beds and close your bedroom door.'

They turned and obeyed her as if in a dream.

She hurried to the outer door, her doll tucked under her arm, turned the key in the lock, and knew she was free. But once outside with the night wind in her hair, she turned back. She tore a sheet of paper from her writing book, covered it with kisses, and laid it on her pillow. She wrote *DAVY* at the top and *LAVER* at the bottom. Then she slipped out into the night, and this time she did not return. With the salt and scent of the sea in her nostrils, she plunged into the water and swam towards home with swift, tireless strokes.

Chapter 9

TWO SAD HEARTS

LAVER'S MEETING WITH her family was something none of them ever forgot. When she saw how thin her mother had become during her absence, and what deep lines of pain and anxiety marked her father's face, she clung to them each in turn, while Emerald and Bubbles flickered round them, asking questions and telling her how they had searched for her, day and night. The little ones were happy too and the baby waved her hands and gave cries like a newly-hatched bird because she was too young to talk.

When it was Laver's turn to talk, while the others listened, she saw surprise—wonder—amazement—grow on their faces. When she described the kindness and gentleness of her captors, the hours Davy spent playing with her and reading to her and teaching her, the midnight swims—their wonder grew.

'But they kept you tied up,' said Bubbles. 'That was nasty of them.'

'Not really. They—they were so fond of me they didn't want to lose me. I was part of the family, a daughter for Patrick and a sister for Davy. Charming them with my harp to let me free was the hardest thing I've ever done.'

'You'd rather have stayed on land,' said Emerald. 'You wish you had.'

Laver's meeting with her family was something none of them ever forgot.

'No—I belong here with you. But—' She hesitated.

'I understand,' said her mother quickly. 'Part of you belonged with them. Not many sea-people have experienced what you have experienced, that close tie with land-beings, with humans.'

'I understand too,' said the Lord of the Sea, in his deep rolling voice. 'But be advised by me, daughter. Take care to have no more dealings with mortals. They are intended to live their lives on the land, as you are intended to live yours in the sea. If you try to mix them, the end is sorrow.'

The end was sorrow indeed in the little white-washed fisherman's hut.

'How could she have got out?' said Davy, again and again. 'How could she have left us? How could she, Father, how could she?'

'I don't know,' said Patrick huskily. 'Someone undid the knots of her harness, even the secret knot that I alone knew how to tie.'

'I'm wondering——' began Davy. 'I think I dreamed of harp music during the night. Do you think someone—some mermaid with a harp—charmed us to set her free? You remember, she told us how her mother played magical music and charmed the sailor, Billy Bones, to leave his ship and his mates and dwell in the depths of the ocean?'

'That's all I can think of, lad. Or she charmed us her-self. But how did she get her harp?'

'Father, do you remember how she snapped at me when I went to get her pillow for her bed? She'd never, not once, spoken to me like that before.'

'I do. Maybe the harp was hidden in the pillow.'

'But she didn't want to go.' Davy looked at the page of kisses for the hundredth time. 'Here's a blur and here and here. She was crying when she made those kisses and wrote the names.'

'Davy, lad, she did what she had to. She went back to her own land and her own people. But it went hard with her, it went hard. She loved you as much as her mermaid's heart would let her. So much, so very much.'

'But not enough,' said Davy. 'Not enough.'

'Love can never be enough between mortals and sea-people,' said his father. 'Never. Take my advice and have no further dealings with those of the watery world. It will end in sorrow.'

'It has,' said Davy. 'My heart is broken.'

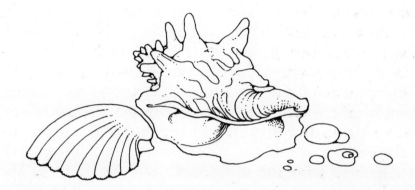

Chapter 10

BUBBLES' SECRET

TIME PASSES UNDER the sea very much as it passes on land. Sometimes it seems to go quickly and sometimes slowly. But the beat of the heart and the tick of the clock remain constant. It just seems that the waters flow quicker—or slower—as the tide turns.

For weeks Laver fretted for the narrow walls of the fisherman's hut, for the kind voices and gentle hands, even for the feel of her harness over her shoulders and round her waist. But gradually she slipped back into the old ways, the ways of the ocean. Her mother often asked her to help with the little ones, and the Lord of the Sea himself took her with him on long, swift journeys through deep and dangerous waters, sometimes to consult with other Lords who lived in remote places.

Then there were Emerald and Bubbles, not as gentle and eager to please as Davy, but full of fun and frolic. Both Emerald and Laver noticed that Bubbles sometimes went away on his own, secretly if he could manage it, but if he were observed, forbidding them to follow.

'Don't dare come after me,' he would say sternly. 'I'll never forgive you if you do. I'll never play with you again.'

'Where does he go? What does he do?' questioned the little mermaids. Bubbles was the oldest in the family and stronger than they, and he had no other merman

48

to share his games. The next brother was still only small, kept in the nursery cave with the other little ones, too tender to be exposed to the perils of the deep. Then, one day, fate revealed Bubbles' secret against his will.

A great storm was blowing on the surface of the ocean, but in the deeps, where the sea-people dwelt, all was calm. They only knew of its fury by the distant echo of its crashing breakers and the way the sea-creatures took refuge at deeper and safer levels. Billy Bones was the only person who was uneasy when a tempest was raging.

'Many a gallant ship will go down, and many a brave lad never see his home again,' he said to himself. 'It's a cruel end for such as choose the sea for their calling, yes, a cruel end.'

Emerald and Laver were swinging happily in the hammock knotted of sea-grass that Billy Bones had made them. No man was ever handier than Billy, whatever the task. As the Mermaid Mother often said, she didn't think she could manage her large family without him. As they swung, they talked of Bubbles and his mysterious absences. But, as usual, neither had any ideas —only wild guesses.

Suddenly, they felt a shadow approaching and saw Bubbles swimming towards them, not swooping through the water like a diving fish, but moving slowly and painfully. He put a finger to his lips, to prevent them crying out with surprise.

They slipped out of their knotted hammock, put their thin arms round him, and laid him in the hammock in

49

their place. His face was deathly pale and his curls lay flat on his head. Then Laver said in a shocked tone:

'Your tail, Bubbles! You're wounded. Oh the blood!'

Emerald looked as well and decided what they must do. Laver was thankful, for once, that Emerald was the elder and could sometimes take the lead.

'Go quickly to the cave for some rolled bandages. And a sponge. Try not to be seen.'

Laver was back very quickly with wide bandages of seaweed, each neatly rolled, and a large sponge. Emerald sponged the deep cut which was about halfway down Bubbles' silver tail. The water all round was tinged with red.

'Press your hands, one each side,' said Emerald to Laver. 'Turn your head away if you feel sick. Just press steadily and firmly. I'll bandage it as tightly as I can.'

Laver pressed and she did feel sick, but she was able to help Emerald to pull the bandage tightly after each turn. Bubbles sat up to watch, brave as a sea-lion, and never uttered a sound, though even his lips were white. When Emerald had finished, the bandage was neat and firm.

'I shall say I cut it on a sharp rock,' said Bubbles presently.

'But you didn't, did you? It was curved. You couldn't have hit yourself hard enough. Unless someone threw a stone at you?'

'No, but I shall have to say something. We must all say the same. Or you needn't say anything—you weren't there.'

50

When Emerald had finished, the bandage was neat and firm.

'The cut reminded me of something,' said Emerald, 'and I can't remember what. But I shall remember soon. I know I shall.'

She remembered in a few minutes and turned to Bubbles who was looking a little better.

'It was like a horse's hoof. The sharp, curved edge of a hoof. Bubbles, you were kicked, that's the truth, isn't it?'

'Isn't it?' echoed Laver.

Bubbles looked as if he were going to deny it, but he changed his mind and said defiantly:

'Well, what if I were kicked? What of it?'

'Oh, Bubbles, you shouldn't have gone near them. You know how often the Lord of the Sea warns us, forbids us to go anywhere near the wild white horses. He says they are so powerful that a child could easily be killed by a flying hoof, or a bite, or be crushed between them. Even a full-grown merman like Father is at risk. How dared you?'

'I've been trying to tame one of them,' explained Bubbles. 'When it's stormy and they come riding in on the breakers, manes and tails streaming, eyes rolling, I've been swimming among them and calling to them. I've stroked a young one, Silverskin, and patted him. He gives a whinny of pleasure.'

'But the danger!' said Laver.

'It's not as bad as you think. They are so big and I seem so small, I can keep near the surface, above them. It's very exciting. I'm far from their hooves.'

'Then how—' began Emerald.

'I was careless. I turned back for home and dived too soon. I'm sure the white horse that kicked me never even knew he'd done it.'

Chapter 11

THE WHITE HORSES

BUBBLES' MOTHER DID not see him till he looked his usual self, except for the bandage, and she congratulated the girls on their skilful work.

But Bubbles had not learned his lesson. When the wound had healed with a horseshoe-shaped scar, he still longed to ride the wild white horses again. When next there was a storm, he slipped away and his sisters were anxious till he returned, this time unharmed.

'I rode one of them,' he boasted happily. 'I rode on his great wide arching back, and clung to his long mane. It was glorious. I'd like to do it every day.'

'How can you guide the horse with no rein?' asked Emerald.

'You can't. That's half the fun. You just grip with your knees and twist your fingers in his mane, and go where he goes and plunge when he plunges. And dive when he dives. You only have to stick on—he does all the rest, and you never know what the next thing will be.'

Bubbles fell into the habit of riding with the wild white horses whenever there was a storm, and though his sisters were always pleased to see him back safely, they almost stopped worrying. He had no more accidents and always came home in high spirits. Their only job was to cover up his absences if their parents asked awkward questions.

'Do you know where Bubbles is? I wanted him to help me to hang some new seaweed curtains. He's never here when there are jobs to be done. Do you know, Laver?'

'No, Mother,' replied Laver truthfully. 'You know how he likes to go off swimming by himself.'

'Yes, he's a strong swimmer,' said the Lord of the Sea, proudly. 'I've taken him with me on some long journeys and he never flags. At the end, he's fitter than me, leaping around like a young dolphin.'

One day a particularly fierce storm blew up. Even the calm depths where the sea-people lived were troubled and the noise of the waves disturbed the little ones. The Mermaid Mother attempted to soothe them with harp music, but she complained that the continual movement of the water untuned her harp. Billy Bones was called in to play his pipe, but the sound of fretful crying continued.

'We must try to stop Bubbles going riding,' whispered Emerald to Laver, but when they searched for him in his usual haunts, he was nowhere to be found.

'Surely he hasn't—' began Emerald.

'Well, he has. He'd never miss a chance like this.'

'When does the tide turn, Father?' asked Laver, some time later.

'Quite soon, less than an hour. Then things may be more peaceful. Your mother hasn't had a minute's rest with the little ones so upset. I'll go and help her.'

'Bubbles often comes home when the tide turns,' Emerald murmured.

But an hour passed, and there was no sign of him. His sisters knew that questions would soon be asked, and they were.

'Do you know where Bubbles is, Laver?'

'I don't *know*,' said Laver.

'Do you know, Emerald?'

'I don't *know*, either.'

Their father looked at them with stern dark eyes.

'But you could make a good guess, is that it?'

The little mermaids hung their heads. They could not meet the direct gaze that seemed to go right through them.

'It is as I thought. I don't encourage you to tell tales on each other, but this is no time to quibble. Bubbles may be in grave danger. Tell me all you know. Leave nothing unsaid.'

Stumbling and hesitating, the two told the story of Bubbles and his passion for riding the wild white horses.

'That wound on his tail was a kick?' said their mother.

'Yes, the only time a hoof has injured him.'

'You should have told us, my daughters,' said their father.

'We did warn him, again and again, but he was so sure of himself. He always came home radiant. He must have become very very skilful as he said he could mount any horse he chose and stay on whatever they did. Don't be too fearful.'

'But this gale is one of the worst I can ever remember. What do you think, Billy Bones?'

'Force Ten gale I reckon,' said Billy Bones. 'Breakers

55

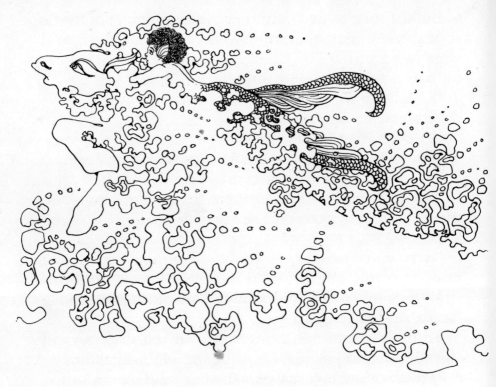

Bubbles loved to ride the wild white horses.

like mountains. I'm sure Bubbles will have his work cut out to ride a wild white horse today.'

'May we go nearer the shore and look for him ourselves?' pleaded Emerald and Laver.

'No, you may not. Nor you either, my love,' said the Lord of the Sea as he saw his wife was preparing to go. 'Billy and I will go as far as is safe, but no further. Two of us lost to the family would be worse even than one. Billy knows so much about the laws of the sea that

I shall be guided by his wisdom and experience. Now go calmly about your duties. We shall need a meal when we return. You children can help to restore order indoors. Much has been shifted and disarranged.'

He kissed his wife and swam off shorewards. His daughters did as they were bidden, but the tears ran down their cheeks as they worked.

At last the two searchers returned, silent and exhausted. The white horses were plunging less madly and turning out to sea, but of Bubbles there was no sign. No sea-bird or sea-creature had seen him.

'The coast is long,' said the Lord of the Sea, 'and he may have been flung ashore far away. Now go to bed and beg Neptune to aid us. Only the gods can help us.'

During the days that followed, the storms gradually died away and when the waters were calmer, the search for Bubbles went on. But the sea stayed choppy and only Billy Bones and the Merman Father could approach the shore and return in safety.

They never gave up hope. There were so many caves and rocky places, under the sea and on the wide shore, where Bubbles could easily be lying, perhaps injured.

'Perhaps dead,' they all thought in their hearts, seeing Bubbles with a great gash among his fair curls. But of this they never spoke, not even to themselves in a whisper.

Chapter *12*

BUBBLES' LAST RIDE

BUBBLES HAD RIDDEN the Force Ten gale with his usual dash and enjoyment. Perhaps the troughs between the waves were deeper, the foaming crests more lofty, but he kept his seat and the crashing and roaring were music in his ears. When the tide turned the wild white horses swung seawards, but the weight of water pushing them shorewards again was very great. They had raced further up the beaches than usual and it was not easy to swing round. The horse Bubbles was riding made several attempts to change direction, and suddenly dived down to turn below the surface. As he dived, he tossed his head and arched his neck, the snowy mane slid from between Bubbles' clutching fingers. He lost his grip and was flung backward on to the shore.

It was not a quiet sandy shore, like the one where they watched the land-children play. It was bounded by a high concrete promenade with railings, and a road behind, and a row of buildings beyond the road. The sea very seldom came over the promenade but this high tide had broken all rules and scattered sand and shingle over the smooth paving.

People were watching the waves, standing in little groups, buttoned into mackintoshes against the shower of spray.

Bubbles was thrown right over the promenade and

Mr and Mrs Grim prodded poor Bubbles.

landed on the road, at the feet of a man and woman.
They both had thin lips and disagreeable expressions.
The man prodded Bubbles with his foot, trying to turn
him over.

'A rum fish, this.'

'I've never seen anything like it in our fish shop,'
said his wife.

'It may be some rare, tropical kind, perhaps we
could sell it to some museum.'

'You're always wondering how you can make money, aren't you? We don't even know if the thing is dead.'

Together they rolled Bubbles on to his back.

'A mermaid!' they exclaimed together. 'A mermaid.'

'There's money in this,' said the man. 'I'll wrap it in my mac and we'll carry it home and see if we can bring it round. There's many a zoo or amusement park that would give a tidy sum for such a curiosity—more if it's alive.'

'And if it's dead?'

'It can be stuffed or something. There's plenty of ideas in my head already. We'll make our fortunes yet.'

When they reached home, they examined Bubbles more carefully. He seemed to be breathing. When they held a mirror in front of his mouth it misted over. He was very cold.

'Let's put her in a warm bath,' said the man.

'But fishes should be cold. They are cold-blooded. Mermaids will be the same.'

'This one wants reviving. Do what I say. Run a warm bath.'

His wife did as she was told and they laid Bubbles in the bath. Now, a warm bath is as unwelcome to a merman as a cold bath would be to a land-child, particularly if he had just had an accident and wasn't feeling well.

Bubbles began to wriggle and writhe in discomfort, giving little moans as if in pain.

'She's alive all right,' said the man, whose name was Mr Grim. 'Listen, she can talk.'

Bubbles was saying faintly but clearly: 'Too hot! Too hot!'

'What did I say? Fishes like to be cold.' Mrs Grim turned on the cold tap, and Bubbles gradually stopped flapping uneasily, and lay still.

'What do we do next?'

'We'll keep her in the bath till we've found a good home for her—at a price. I'll draw the curtains and we'll lock her in. Now not a word to anyone. She must be our secret. Remember that, Dotty. No tittle-tattle to the neighbours. I've a lot of planning to do—and telephoning.'

It was a very good thing that Bubbles, locked in the bathroom, could hear nothing that went on downstairs. If he had, he wouldn't have drifted comfortably off to sleep, the bath sponge behind his head for a pillow.

It was nearly midnight when Mr Grim laid down the telephone and wiped his forehead.

'I've struck a bargain,' he said contentedly. 'I've sold her to the Zodiac Zoo. That is, of course, when the zoo people have seen her and satisfied themselves she's all I've cracked her up to be. And we know she is.'

'How will you get her there? We can't fit the bath into the fish van,' said Mrs Grim.

'It's only a two-hour drive along the highway. If we wrap her round in wet bath towels I reckon she'll survive. They are preparing a tank where she can be on display. They'll make it attractive with shells and seaweed and things. She'll be the draw of the season. They'll charge

61

an extra fee to visit the mermaid—twenty pence or more. They'll make a mint of money that way.'

'And what do we get?'

'Fifty pounds if we deliver her alive and well.'

'Couldn't you have asked more?' said Mrs Grim, who was as money-loving as her husband.

'I tried, but the zoo people wouldn't go any higher.'

'Well, fifty pounds for something washed up by the high tide is pretty good. She hasn't cost us a penny. I'll try her with a tasty fish-paste sandwich before we go to bed.'

But Bubbles was too tired and sleepy to eat and wouldn't open his eyes or his mouth, so Mrs Grim ate the sandwich herself. It was a pity to waste good food, as she remarked with her mouth full.

Chapter 13

ZODIAC ZOO

ALTHOUGH BUBBLES HAD only been one night in the Grim household he was already sure that he had not been as fortunate as Laver with her fisherfolk. She spoke continually of their gentle voices and loving ways, and how they did everything in their power to please her. Mr and Mrs Grim were not gentle. Their voices were harsh and their touch rough. When they lifted him out of the bath and wrapped him in wet towels their sharp fingers nipped him like a crab's claws and when he slipped on the wet bathroom floor, Mr Grim snapped 'Stand up, can't you?' and gave him an angry shake.

If he had not hit his head so violently on the hard road, Bubbles would have been able to think more clearly, but his mind was in a daze. He would have tried, straight away, to escape from these people who frightened him. There was the bathroom window with a convenient drainpipe down which he might have climbed. There were other possibilities, too, but with his aching head and feelings of sickness and dizziness, plans were impossible to make, as impossible as fish-paste sandwiches were to eat. He longed only for sleep and even then there was a beating in his ears and sharp jabs of pain.

Although Bubbles felt more like himself the next day,

he also felt more trapped, and he disliked everything about Mr and Mrs Grim. He disliked their voices, their rough touch, the way they spoke continually of money, and the smell of them made him feel sick. Sea-people, if they smell of anything, smell fresh and faintly salty. These land-people smelt stuffy and unpleasant. And the air he breathed on the highway reeked of fumes. He arrived at the Zodiac Zoo more dead than alive.

The keeper of the zoo was a huge man who always carried a whip. The few animals in the dirty cramped cages looked in poor condition, some with their fur coming out in patches and all with dull, sad eyes. Bubbles knew at a glance that they were unhappy. He longed to set them all free. But alas, he was a prisoner himself, and would soon be in need of someone to set *him* free.

They went into a dark room with a stone floor, and a glass tank at one end, brightly lit. There were railings in front to keep people from touching the glass.

'Unwrap her,' said Mr Bellow, the man with the whip. 'Let me see what she can do. Drop her in the tank where I can see her. I'm not paying good money for anything except the best.'

Even Mr and Mrs Grim were over-awed by this giant of a man and hastened to undo the towels and throw Bubbles into the tank, which was to be his home.

At once he began to dive and feel the extent of his prison with his hands. It was very very small. Two strokes one way and one the other. That was all the swimming he could do without hitting the sides. The seaweed was made of brilliantly coloured plastic, orange

and blue and magenta, and the shells and stones were
not real either. All were manufactured. There was nothing to remind him of his old home except the water, and
that was too salty for comfort.

'At least they made it salty because they thought I
should like it,' he thought mournfully. 'They were trying to please me, or I suppose they were.'

'Very pretty little mermaid, better than I expected,'
purred Mr Bellow. 'What does she eat?'

'Anything,' said Mrs Grim quickly. She was not going
to lose £50 because of the faddiness of a fish. Anyhow,
the mermaid would eat anything if it was hungry
enough.

Mr Bellow counted out some crumpled notes and Mr
Grim stowed them away in his wallet. Then the Grims
departed. The last Bubbles heard was the two voices
quarrelling over the merits of a new carpet or a weekend
in Spain.

'You're not half bad,' said Mr Bellow, giving
Bubbles' curls a sharp painful tug. 'You're a proper
mermaid.'

'But I'm not,' said Bubbles. 'I'm a MERMAN. A
boy. Mermen have silver tails and short curly hair.
Mermaids have green tails and long straight hair. And
they can play the harp. Though of course they have to
be taught.'

Mr Bellow's face went pale. He cracked his whip in
a way that made Bubbles shiver.

'Now listen to me, mermaid, and listen carefully. If
you say one single word to anyone who comes to see you,

Mr Bellow counted out some crumpled notes.

you'll get a taste of my whip. And that's an experience you won't want twice, I can tell you. Remember—not a single word—ever—to the public. Or you'll suffer for it. You'll wish you'd never been born. You can talk to me if you like, when the public has gone home and the Zoo's closed for the night. Understand?'

'Yes,' said Bubbles. 'But why mustn't I speak to any of the—of the public?'

'Because they'll think you're a fraud. They'll think you're a child or a midget or something, dressed up in a mermaid's costume. It's what I'd think myself in their place.'

'But you know I'm not a child dressed up, and you know I can talk. What do you think, Mr Bellow?'

'I'm jiggered if I know what to think. But you'll be a little gold mine.' He rubbed his hands with delight, muttering 'A real live mermaid. Who'd have believed it possible?'

'Only I'm not a mermaid,' repeated Bubbles timidly. 'I'm a merman.'

'You're a mermaid and that's all there is to it. I'm having the bills printed at the moment:

'ONLY REAL LIVE MERMAID IN THE WORLD'
'COME AND SEE FOR YOURSELVES'

'Oh, but—' began Bubbles.

'Now don't you dare "oh but" me. I don't like being contradicted. No one ever does contradict me.' He glared round the zoo with its shabby cages and sad-eyed animals. He cracked his whip, and the animals cowered in the darkest corners they could find.

'Now you know what's what, mermaid? The public come in at ten in the morning, and I lock the gates at seven in the evenings, except on Saturdays. Then I keep open as long as people keep coming. While there's anybody in the Mermaid's Cave—that's what I'm going to call this room you're in—I shall have it written over the door—you must swim and dive and bob about. Look lively, in fact. If there's no one near, you can rest or sleep or whatever you please. But no slacking mind you. All my animals have to earn their keep and so must you.'

'Supposing I get tired and lie down for five minutes, what will happen? Why should the public mind?'

'I have a rather nasty way of waking up lazy animals,' said Mr Bellow. 'Of course the public doesn't want to see you sleep. You mightn't even be alive—you might be stuffed.'

'Wouldn't I be interesting if I were stuffed?' asked Bubbles.

'No. You'd be boring. Deadly dull, in fact. Dead stuffed things are in museums. Live things are in zoos. That's the difference. Now this is our half day and the zoo is closed. So you can amuse yourself until tomorrow morning. Someone'll be bringing you your supper. Bye-bye, mermaid.'

Chapter 14

ENTER SID

THE NEXT FEW hours were the longest Bubbles had ever known. Mr Bellow had turned off the bright lights round the tank to save electricity, which was a relief, but Bubbles' head still ached from the bang it had when he was flung on shore, on to the hard road. He tried to settle in his new home and to get some sleep, but there seemed no way of getting comfortable. The plastic sea-weed, which was somehow stuck to the glass, was prickly and scratched him. The stones were sharp too, not like the rounded stones at the bottom of the sea, which had been tossed and turned and rolled around till they were smooth as could be. He tried to go to sleep floating, but the water was not deep enough to support him. He twisted and wriggled and tried one position and then another, but it was no use.

'I wonder if I shall die from lack of sleep,' he thought to himself. 'It would be better than living in this miserable tank.'

Just then he heard footsteps and a clattering noise outside. The door of the Mermaid's Cave opened, someone switched on the electric lights, and Bubbles saw a freckled face smiling at him. He smiled back and said:

'Who are you?'

There was an even louder clatter as the freckled boy dropped the bucket he was carrying.

69

'I'm Sid, the odd-job boy. The boss never told me he had a talking mermaid in here. I've brought your supper. Are you feeling peckish?'

'What is my supper, please?'

'Fish. You can have as much as you like. The sea-lion didn't fancy his, so you can have it.'

'It smells rather—rather strong,' said Bubbles anxiously. 'And I don't care for eating fish. I was brought up to be friendly to fish. I couldn't possibly eat one.'

'These are a bit niffy, I agree,' said Sid. 'But fish soon goes off. The boss didn't say what else you could have.'

'Something green and fresh. Like seaweed,' suggested Bubbles.

'I can bring you a lettuce. Our tortoise is off his feed too. Would you like to try that?'

'Yes please.'

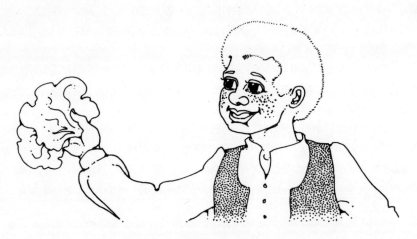

Sid brought Bubbles some lettuce.

Bubbles managed to nibble a leaf or two and felt better. He didn't know if it was his supper or Sid's smiling face that had done him good. When Mr Bellow did his round he found Bubbles snuggled up in a corner, his curly hair pillowed on his silver tail, fast asleep.

'I hope the mermaid thrives,' said Mr Bellow to himself. 'No fish—that's bad. But I suppose there's some goodness in a lettuce leaf. Now if only a hundred people come to see her tomorrow that'll be ...' He spent the rest of the evening doing sums. There was no doubt in his mind that if the mermaid lived, he would make his fortune. If she only lived for a year, he wouldn't do badly. Alas, Mr Bellow had known only too many animals who hadn't lived a year—many not a month, others not a week—and some only a day. You couldn't say that he had a way with animals.

Chapter 15

THE ZOO OPENS

THE NEXT DAY at ten o'clock, Sid unlocked the gates of the Zodiac Zoo. There was not the rush of people waiting to come in that Mr Bellow had dreamed of, but several families with children were ready to pay entrance money, and more drove up soon after. Almost all of them immediately saw the large notice about the mermaid:

'*THE ONLY REAL MERMAID IN THE WORLD*'

The children clamoured to see her and begged their parents to pay the extra twenty pence that would admit them to the Mermaid's Cave.

'Oh, Dad, a real mermaid. I'd rather see her than have a ride on the camel, or have an ice-cream.'

'Look! Those other children are buying tickets. There'll be a queue soon. Mum wants to see her, don't you, Mum?'

'What is a mermaid?' asked one of the little ones. 'Is it fierce and wild?'

It was the fathers who were not as enthusiastic as their families.

'It'll be a fake. You see, it'll be a fake. Some poor child holding a harp and pretending to be a mermaid, with a tail covered with tinfoil and a long blonde wig.

I just don't believe in mermaids, any more than I believe in fairies or witches. And it all costs money.'

'Even if she is a fake mermaid,' said one of the older children, 'and I think she's a real one, let's go and see how they've faked her. You see if you can spot the wig and the tinfoil and all the other tricks. You see if you can catch them out, Dad.'

In the end, most of the children got their own way and nobody was disappointed, except the few grown-ups who had expected—even hoped— that the exhibit would be disappointing. Then they could complain and perhaps even get their money back.

The day seemed endless for Bubbles, as did all the days that followed. The lights made his eyes ache and he longed for a cool swim in the shadowy depths where he had once lived. He felt cramped and confined, and though, for a few minutes, the public interested him, the interest soon wore off. The water in his tank grew uncomfortably warm and smelt stale and unpleasant, in spite of the salt that had been added.

There was a notice saying:

'DO NOT FEED THIS MERMAID'

But all kinds of unappetising things were thrown in. Sticky licorice all-sorts, crumbs of biscuit. Even bits of chewing gum. Bubbles did not attempt to eat any of them. The smell was enough. After a few days Mr Bellow and Sid fixed a cover of wire-netting over the top of the tank which prevented all these unwelcome offerings from getting into the water.

Bubbles stuck to his diet of lettuces and Mr Bellow sometimes added watercress and half a grapefruit on Sundays. These Bubbles enjoyed. He pitied the poor sea-lion with its rotting smelly fish and was not surprised when Sid told him, one day, that it had died.

'Mr Bellow is very cross,' added Sid.

'Isn't he upset and sorry?'

'He's only upset because he gave a lot of money for the sea-lion and now it's dead he reckons he'll lose a lot. The public like to see a sea-lion dive off a rock, just as they like to see you swimming about. Mr Bellow thinks you're a great success and he's very pleased with you. But he said the other day that you weren't quite as lively as when you first came.'

'I don't feel at all lively,' said Bubbles. 'There's nothing to be lively about. No one to play with. No one to talk to.'

'You've got me,' said Sid sadly, 'but I know I'm not a mermaid.'

'Oh, Sid,' said Bubbles quickly. 'You're my best friend. My only friend. How could I forget? I'd pine away and die if you weren't here.'

'Hurry up there, lazybones!' came Mr Bellow's gruff voice. 'Don't take all day to feed the mermaid. I hope she's quite well,' he added suspiciously. 'Let's have a look at her.'

His way of having a look was to remove the cover and grab Bubbles' curls and haul him out of the water to inspect him. This was painful and Bubbles twisted and squirmed which delighted Mr Bellow.

'Don't take all day to feed the mermaid,' said Mr Bellow.

'Plenty of life in this mermaid,' he said approvingly. 'Plenty of life. She's flourishing. You may give her half a grapefruit for supper even if it isn't Sunday.'

Bubbles hardly looked at the public after a while. They all seemed much the same, laughing, joking, babies crying, children eating sweets and asking questions. Occasionally a soft voice, or a gentle 'Isn't she beautiful?', made him look up, and sometimes a complaint—'That tank isn't big enough, the poor thing can hardly swim at all'—made him give a grateful look.

Chapter 16

TWO VISITORS

BUT ONE DAY two visitors who came to the Mermaid's Cave drew Bubbles' attention at once. This was not because they were noisy, or pushing, or wearing outlandish clothes. It was because they were so quiet and ordinary. They seemed to be father and son, as their sunburned faces were rather alike. They were wearing navy blue knitted jerseys and dark trousers. They did not speak, just gazed at Bubbles with great concentration.

Without pushing, they waited patiently till they reached the iron railing that kept people from actually touching the glass tank. There they stayed for many minutes, never taking their eyes off Bubbles. Then the boy said firmly:

'It's a merman all right, Father. There's no deception.'

'You're right, Davy. How it brings her back to mind! The greenish hands.'

'The swish of the tail.'

'The shining green eyes.'

'And what's more, I think it must be her brother Bubbles. She said he had short golden curls and a silvery tail, and their faces are so alike.'

'Yes, they're like twins. But remember we haven't seen other mermaids or mermen. Perhaps they *are* all very like each other.'

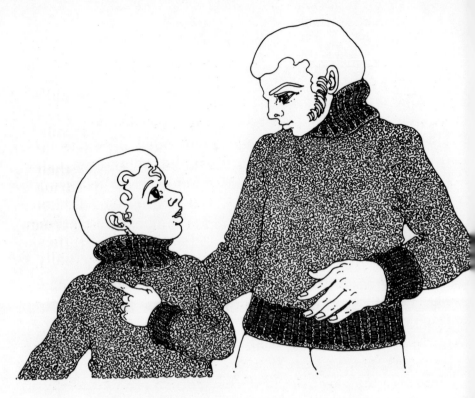

'It's a merman all right, Father,' said Davy.

'Let's wait till there's a chance of speaking to him.
The crowd is leaving. It's nearly closing time. We shan't
have to wait long.'

The people were leaving the Cave and soon there
were only the two dark figures of father and son left.

'Now,' said Davy. 'Now's your chance.'

His father leaned over the iron bar till his face was
near the glass of the tank. At the same moment, Bubbles
pressed his face against his side of the glass.

'Are you Bubbles?' asked Patrick.

'Yes, yes I am.'

'We are Patrick and Davy. We knew and loved your sister Laver. We love her still.'

'She spoke only good of you,' said Bubbles. 'Please save me for her sake. I have a most miserable life here. Please help me.'

'We will. Truly we will. But it may take time. We shall have to make a plan. Keep cheerful. We'll rescue you somehow, I promise.'

'And so do I,' added Davy. 'We'll save you, never fear.'

Just then there was a heavy step behind them and Mr Bellow came in.

'Talking to the mermaid, are you?' he growled suspiciously.

'He doesn't understand us,' laughed Patrick. 'It's just my son. You know the way children talk to cats—and birds—and anything that's alive. Silly, but childish.'

'Why did you say "he"?' asked Mr Bellow.

'Did I?' said Patrick calmly. 'He—she—it—they're all the same to me. I must congratulate you on your interesting collection of animals. And the mermaid is the pick of the bunch. Well worth an extra twenty pence. Never seen anything like it in my life. I wouldn't have believed it possible if I hadn't seen it with my own eyes.'

'Closing time—all out—closing time,' cried Sid, rattling his keys and hustling any lingerers out.

'We shall have to come again,' said Patrick.

'Yes, we must,' said Davy. 'We simply must.'

They allowed Sid to hustle them through the gate marked EXIT.

'There go two satisfied customers,' said Mr Bellow. 'Said they'd come again. Funny that the man said "he" when he mentioned the mermaid.'

'People mostly call her it,' said Sid. 'Never having seen one before they don't know what to call her. How could they?'

'I expect you're right. I'll go into my room and count today's takings. All the mermaid's money should have put them up.' He went off chuckling to himself and rubbing his hands. Counting the money was the most enjoyable part of his day.

In the meantime, Patrick and Davy were going back to their village in the coach that they had caught there in the morning. Patrick had heard, by chance, someone in the post office saying that she'd heard there was a real live mermaid in the Zodiac Zoo. When he repeated this to Davy, Davy had become terribly excited and said they must go and see her.

'Probably a fake,' said his father.

'Then we are the very best people to see if she is real. We're probably the only people who'll ever visit the zoo who have seen a real mermaid. When can we go?'

'I can't say straight off. Other people in the post office were saying that there was occasionally a coach trip to the Zodiac Zoo, I don't know if there'll be one soon. We'll ask the post office lady.'

Luck was on their side and they learned that the

coach was arranged for the week after next. Davy could hardly bear to wait. He counted the days and even attempted to count the hours.

'Supposing the mermaid is Laver, what do we do?'

'If it's a mermaid at all and not some dressed-up thing made to look like a mermaid. Such deceptions are common. And as we know there are countless mermaids in the sea, it isn't likely the very one that may have been captured is Laver. Now is it? Be reasonable.'

'No, it isn't,' agreed Davy. 'It would be another one. But I want to see her just the same. Don't you?'

'Yes, I do,' agreed Patrick. 'Having Laver living with us has completely changed my view on mermaids.'

Chapter 17

THE SLEEPING DRAUGHT

ON THE WAY home in the coach Davy wanted to talk about Bubbles all the time, as he could think of nothing else, but Patrick frowned and shook his head.

'Not a word about what we've seen, Davy, till we're back in the cottage with the door shut. Not a word. If anyone else heard us, it might wreck any plans we could make, and it'll be hard enough, heaven knows, to do what we must. Talk about the other exhibits, if you like.'

So Davy confined himself to odd remarks about the sad face of the little grey monkey and the probable age of the tortoise.

'I liked that freckled boy who took the money and told us when it was time to go,' Davy added.

'So did I,' agreed Patrick. 'We might get him on our side.'

When they were safe home, drinking mugs of cocoa, Davy said:

'Let's start planning.'

'I think we should have a night's rest,' said his father.

'But I'll never sleep a wink till we've talked a little. I know I won't. What's your idea, Father?'

'One of the problems is transport,' said Patrick. 'I'm not sure that it isn't the main problem. We can't just run out of the Zoo with Bubbles in my arms. We'd never get far.'

They talked well into the night and decided that they must borrow a van belonging to another fisherman, called Joe. It was the only van in the little cluster of cottages.

'We can't plan further than that,' said Patrick. 'The van'll get us to the Zoo. We'll arrive near opening time and then we'll see how the land lies. We may be able to get that cheerful, freckled boy, Sid, to help us. Or at least to give a message to Bubbles.'

Joe was willing to lend his van for a day, as Patrick had often done him a good turn in the past, and Davy was thankful that his father could drive. They took a few tools and their treasured green coverlet, which might be useful to roll round Bubbles. It had a silky fringe and a deep border of golden leaves. Also a large sack, which Patrick lined as well as he could with a sheet, and another sack which they intended to fill with newly cut hay. Last of all, after a particularly good catch of fish, Patrick walked to the next village where there was an old woman, some said a witch, but all agreed exceptionally wise and skilled in many unusual arts.

Patrick ploughed his way through the thistles and nettles that grew over her garden path, and knocked on the ricketty door.

'Come in,' croaked a quavering voice.

Patrick went in.

'What is your need?' enquired the old woman.

'I have heard about your great skill at making—er, wine,' began Patrick. 'I wondered if I could buy a bottle.'

83

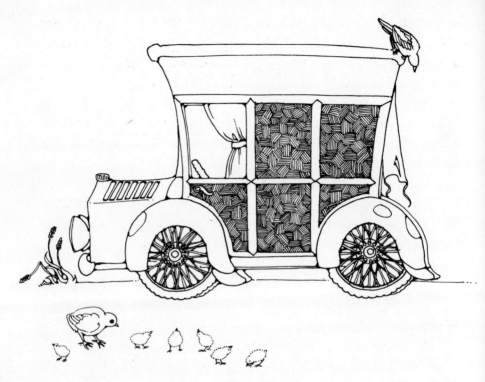

Joe's van.

'I make nothing but healthful potions from the simple plants that grow in the countryside for all to gather, if they wish. Dandelion and elder, rosehip, heather and sloe and wild carrot.'

'I am in great need of some potion which induces sleep,' said Patrick.

'Would it be for a man, woman or child?' asked the Wise Woman.

'A man. Have you such a potion?'

'Yes indeed. Here it is,' and she picked up a bottle

of green liquid. 'A glass of this will bring sleep to the most wakeful mortal. It is made from soothing syrups and I have hobbled many miles to collect all the necessary plants, and then sat up all night long, brewing and simmering and straining.'

'If—if the person were to exceed the dose and in desperation drink two glasses, would it injure his health?'

'If this should happen, have no fear. All my potions cure, none of them injures. He will just sleep the deeper and the longer. But it is not cheap to buy,' she added, eyeing Patrick's darned jersey and patched trousers.

'How much, Ma'am?'

'One pound.'

Patrick took the money from his pocket and gave it to her.

'It is a pound well spent.'

'You'll never regret it, that I swear.' She wiped the bottle on her apron and gave it to him.

Patrick carried it carefully home and put it on a high shelf.

Two days later, Joe drove his van round to the cottage, and early the next morning they set out, the various things they needed stowed in the back. Patrick drove slowly and carefully, as he was out of practice. The unlined sack was full to bursting with the freshest greenest grasses and clovers they could find. This was to be a present for Mr Bellow to put him in a good mood.

'Won't those poor, half-starved animals enjoy all that green stuff?' said Davy, his eyes shining. 'It'll be a real treat after that dry hay and faded lettuce and smelly cabbage.'

'We'll hope so,' said Patrick, who was doubtful about the whole expedition and only too aware of the risks and dangers.

Chapter 18

THE SECOND VISIT

WHEN THEY REACHED Zodiac Zoo the gates were just being unlocked. They parked the van and paid the entrance money, Patrick carrying the sack. Then, from the office, Mr Bellow appeared, whip in hand as usual, and a very disagreeable expression on his fat red face.

'What's going on here?' he shouted, poking the sack with his whip. 'What do you two think you're doing?'

Patrick kept calm and replied in a quiet voice:

'I was hoping I'd see you to explain, Mr Bellow. My lad and I have been to your zoo and were so impressed that we've come a second time. We noticed that some of your animals appeared to relish green stuff, and as we live in the country we filled a sack with tasty fresh greenery as a little present for you. Nothing that could harm a fly, I swear. See for yourself.'

He loosened the mouth of the sack and showed all the grass and clover.

Mr Bellow actually smiled as he thrust his hand into the sack.

'Now I take that as a very kindly thought, very kindly indeed. Just what some of my animals need. The tortoise is still off his feed, and I notice you've included some dandelions. He's very partial to a fresh dandelion leaf, is my tortoise. Thank you both.' His way of thanking

87

Davy was to give him a smart slap on the back, which made him feel sick.

'Come here, Sid,' he called and Sid came hurrying up. Like the animals, he found it best to obey Mr Bellow.

'Don't give away all this good fresh stuff in one meal,' Mr Bellow ordered. 'That would be a waste of good food. Just scatter a few handfuls on top of their usual rations. And see that the tortoise has some of the dandelion leaves. He lives on air, that tortoise.'

'Mr Bellow,' said Patrick respectfully, 'would it be possible for my little lad to go round with Sid when feeding time comes? It would be a treat. And he wouldn't try to go into any of the cages or be a nuisance. Just to watch would be enough.'

'I see no objection,' said Mr Bellow grandly.

'Thank you, Sir, thank you very much, Sir.'

'Sid will call you when he does the feeding. Now don't forget, Sid. This little lad may accompany you, just this once.'

The morning passed and Sid fed some of the smaller animals. Then Patrick paid the entrance money for the Mermaid's Cave. Bubbles was huddled up in a corner looking thin and wretched: even his curls seemed flatter, and the silvery scales on his tail were dull.

'Look lively,' begged Sid. 'You know the boss hates to see you drooping and sulking, and you know how he wakens up droopy animals.'

'I do indeed,' said Bubbles, swimming a few feeble strokes. Mr Bellow had a stick with a sharp nail on the end, and made a habit of jabbing it painfully into any animal who wasn't, in his opinion, showing off to the public.

Then Bubbles saw Patrick and Davy and was transformed in an instant, darting and diving, twisting and turning, as well as he could in his narrow glass prison.

'You've come to save me?' he whispered.

Just then Mr Bellow strode into the Mermaid's Cave and was delighted to see the mermaid so lively. He had feared she was what he called 'going off'. So many animals 'went off' for no reason at all.

'What's livened her up, Sid?' he enquired.

'I gave her a bunch of mares' tails that were in the sack. They grow in water, and I think they just suit her, p'raps they remind her of real seaweed.'

'Anyhow, they've done her a power of good. I'll go off and have my dinner now. Keep your eyes open and don't let anyone slip in without paying.'

Just as Mr Bellow was leaving, Patrick produced the Wise Woman's green bottle.

'Excuse me taking the liberty, Sir, but we're from the country, as I said before, and I've ventured to bring you a bottle of home-made wine. You might care to sup it with your dinner. It's known to be very thirst-quenching and this is a warm day.'

'I usually have beer,' said Mr Bellow. 'But I don't mind trying a glass. Thank you again.'

I hope they aren't up to any tricks, he thought to himself. First the sack of greenstuff. Now the home-made wine. He looked carefully at Patrick and Davy. They appear simple enough, he concluded. Too simple to be up to anything. And there's Sid on duty. And I'll be on duty myself in less than an hour.

But this was where Mr Bellow was wrong. Long before an hour had passed, with four glasses of home-made wine inside him, he was in a deep sleep. Nothing, whether thunder or a lion roaring, could rouse him. And nothing did. He snored so loudly that he could be heard outside his office door. Patrick and Davy rejoiced to hear the sound.

Chapter 19

TWO ESCAPES

THINGS WERE FAIRLY quiet at the Zoo just then. The visitors were picnicking, or buying sweets and ginger-nuts at the little shop, and the Mermaid's Cave was empty of anyone except Patrick, his son and Bubbles.

'Call Sid,' said Patrick to Davy. 'Bring him here.'

Sid was with them in a minute, looking surprised.

'Now listen carefully, Sid,' said Patrick. 'We know this mermaid—well, he's really a merman—and he's ill and miserable. We are going to take him back to the sea where he belongs, and you must help him. We'll take the netting off the top of the tank and put him in a sack I've brought—carry him to the van—and speed off. How do you keep the public out of the Cave while we're working?'

'I could put *Closed for Repairs*,' said Sid. 'But what about Mr Bellow? He'd kill me if he found out.'

'But he won't find out. We gave him some drugged wine that will keep him asleep till tomorrow. Will you help us?'

'Please, please help, Sid. You're my only friend here,' begged Bubbles.

'I'd like to help,' said Sid. 'But I daren't. The boss is sure to find out the mermaid's gone when he wakes up, and there's only me to blame. I can imagine him cracking that whip now.' He shuddered.

'Sid,' said Davy, 'do you like being a zoo boy, always in fear of Mr Bellow and his bad temper and his whip?'

'You're sorry for lots of the animals who are fretting and sick, that I know,' said Bubbles. 'You often do things to help them secretly. Isn't that true?'

'It's true, all right,' said Sid. 'I've often thought of running away, but I don't get paid much and I shouldn't get far. Mr Bellow keeps a bloodhound tied up, and he'd soon track me down.'

'What would you choose to do if you could do anything in the world?' asked Patrick.

The answer came instantly.

'I'd go to sea. I'd be a cabin boy. I'd have run away long ago, but I don't know how to get to the sea.'

'Your dream can come true,' said Patrick. 'We didn't walk here, you know—we *drove* all the way from the coast. Come back with us. Mr Bellow will never catch our van, and the bloodhound won't be able to track you either. I've many good friends among the skippers of boats, up and down the coast, and they're always on the look-out for a lively lad with a taste for the sea. I'll get you fixed up in a few days, and kitted out as well. You'll not need much and the skipper may help. Sea-boots and thick jerseys and first-class oilskins. It's the life for a man.'

Sid's pale, freckled face shone with excitement. So much was happening so quickly that he hardly knew if he were asleep or awake. He shook Patrick's large brown hand again and again, saying thank you, thank you, thank you.

'Now we've work to be done,' said Patrick. 'Write that notice, Sid, saying the Mermaid's Cave is closed for repairs, and pin it on the door. You, Davy, run to the van and fetch my tools and the spare sack.'

The boys did what they were told quickly and Patrick prised the netting off the top of the tank. Then he lifted Bubbles out and lowered him gently into the sack with the smooth, sheet lining, and laid him on the back seat of the van.

The regular sound of Mr Bellow's snores could be heard whenever they were near the office door. This gave Sid courage as he knew he was safe, at least for the present.

Then they hurried to the van. Davy sat with Bubbles and held him steady, and Sid sat next to Patrick. He turned his head for a last look at the zoo where he had worked so hard and been so unhappy.

'Goodbye for ever,' he murmured, and then fixed his eyes on the road ahead, leading to the sea, and the future.

When at last they arrived at the little village, Patrick dropped the two boys and Bubbles at his own cottage and returned the van to Joe.

Bubbles could hardly move round the room, he had become so weak after his confinement in the tank. His muscles had not been properly exercised by swimming as there was barely room for him to do two strokes. The

Patrick lifted Bubbles out of the tank.

two boys helped him and he soon became stronger. He
was delighted to recognise objects that Laver had described.

'That's her bed,' he said, looking at the couch: 'And
her pillow'—touching the cushion: 'And the rocking
chair where she used to rock. Where are her marbles?'

Davy took the old red purse out of a jug on the mantelpiece and opened it. There were six marbles inside.

'She was clever at marbles,' he said. 'She won six off

me. I've never had the heart to play with them since she left. You can take them back to her, if you like.'

'Thank you,' said Bubbles. 'I know she'd love to have them and she'll teach me to play. Perhaps I shall win some for myself.'

Just then Patrick came in and put the kettle on.

'When may I go home, Patrick?'

'Directly your strength has come back. I should think a night's rest will put you right. Then you can swim off first thing in the morning, on the ebb tide. Can you wait till then?'

'Of course I can,' said Bubbles. 'I like being here, Laver told me so much about it, I don't feel strange. Or not very. Look! The kettle's boiling! She told me about the kettle and how you made tea out of it. I almost feel as if I've been here before, Laver described it all so well. Yes, I'd like to have milk. Laver said she liked milk better than tea.'

So Bubbles chattered on, happy to see how human beings lived on shore, and happy to see all he had had to imagine until now, and excited, underneath, to know that the very next day he would be off to his own home and his own family, in the depths of the cool green sea.

Chapter 20

A NIGHT IN THE HUT

PATRICK AND DAVY, especially Davy, were reminded of Laver continually by Bubbles' voice and his way of moving and smiling. They were pleased, too, that they'd made Laver as happy as was possible and that she had talked about them with such affection.

When Bubbles went to bed on the couch he stroked the green silk coverlet they spread over him.

'Laver said it was one of your treasures,' he remarked, 'and thought it was very kind of you to spare it for her.' He fingered the silky fringe.

Davy said: 'But she always longed for her real home with you and cherished anything that reminded her of it. She wouldn't settle at night without the doll we gave her snuggled beside her, like her one at home.'

'She has them both now,' said Bubbles.

In the morning, when Bubbles had had a long sleep, they all had breakfast and went down to the shore. 'We'll row you a little way out,' said Patrick.

He rowed a few yards and then Sid and Davy helped Bubbles over the edge of the boat.

With many goodbyes and waves of his greenish hands, he disappeared. Davy watched till there was no more to see, not even the glint of a silver tail.

Meanwhile Sid was looking out to the horizon and wondering how soon he would find a skipper who would let him 'join' his boat. Mr Bellow and his dreary zoo seemed far, far away.

In a few days Sid found himself signed on with a kindly skipper, rigged out in sailor's clothes, and a member of the crew (the youngest and smallest) of *The Ocean Wave*.

Patrick and Davy went back to their usual work of catching fish, though Davy felt unsettled and discontented. His few hours with Bubbles had brought back the memories of Laver that he was at last beginning to push aside. Now they were fresh once more and he lived over the few weeks she had spent with them again and again. The games they had played. The talks they had had. The moonlit swims when the shore was deserted. Her golden hair that she combed daily with his old comb. He had to accept, once more, that she was a sea-creature and must live in the sea, just as he was a land-child and must live on land.

Patrick understood why Davy had become moody and silent.

'It will pass,' he said in his comforting voice. 'And now you know from what Bubbles told us that Laver really enjoyed her life with us. I shouldn't be surprised if she, too, had a hard time, getting used to her old home and her own family.'

'You think she may have felt homesick for me?' said Davy.

'I do. Just as you are homesick for her.'

Davy found this idea very consoling, and soon he began to be his own, cheerful self, whistling to the seagulls.

Chapter 21

BACK HOME

DOWN IN THE deep caverns where the purple seaweed grew, Bubbles was being welcomed by his family, especially by his sister Laver. He had to tell the tale of his adventures many times, as the little ones who shuddered at Mr Bellow and his 'whip' begged to hear the whole story all over again when he got to the end. Laver liked to listen too, but she liked even better to hear about Davy and his father and their little hut on the shore. She kept questioning him about things she remembered. 'Did they give you the flowery cup? And cover you with the green silk bedspread? And was your pillow very soft? And did you have bread and honey?'

'Oh stop worrying me,' said Bubbles after several days of her questions. 'I was only in the hut for one night. You were there for weeks and weeks. Of course I can't remember as much as you.'

Then, seeing her face fall, he added, 'But I was there long enough to see what a nice boy Davy was, I'd like him for my brother if he could be changed into a merman. Now show me how to play marbles. Perhaps in time I'll win some of your six for myself.'

The Lord of the Sea was a person of few words. He laid his hand on Bubbles' shoulder and said:

'You were a very very foolish boy and it's only the

98

courage and kindness of two human beings who saved you from a life in that horrible tank. I hope you have learned your lesson.'

'Yes, Father,' said Bubbles, 'but it was *three* human beings, Sid was brave too.'

The Mermaid Mother looked sad when she heard Bubbles and Laver talking about the fisherman's hut. She thought she hated the fisherfolk beyond all, but how could she when they had shown such kindness and gentleness to her own children? Her mind was divided.

'Do you want to go and live with Patrick and Davy?' she asked. 'Is that what you really want?'

'Oh no, Mother,' they said, throwing their arms round her neck and kissing her. 'Oh no, never. We couldn't *live* on shore. You are our mother and this is our home.'

'But they were kind,' added Laver.

'Yes, they were,' agreed Bubbles. 'We wouldn't be back with you without their help.'

Their mother sighed, and stroked the two golden heads, one curly and one straight. She hoped her children would always stay by her side.

Emerald said the least, but she thought the most, and her thoughts were not all happy ones. She loved Laver and Bubbles, and was glad both were safely home, but she was jealous that they had had so many adventures, and attracted so much notice now they were back. When Bubbles told the little ones—for the fiftieth time—how he had been sold to Mr Bellow and put in a glass tank in a zoo, every fish and crab from far and

Even the shrimps clustered around Laver to listen.

wide gathered round to hear. It was the same if Laver described how she had lived in the fisherman's hut. Even the shrimps clustered around her to listen.

The Mermaid Mother noticed the envious expression on Emerald's face and tried to put things right.

'Father and I value you specially, my darling, because you did not disobey us and cause us anxiety and sorrow. Soon even the little ones will get weary of hearing the stories of zoos and fishermen's huts and all will be forgotten. Come with me and have your harp lesson.

You know how useful Laver found her harp when she needed to charm Patrick and Davy.'

'I don't want a harp lesson,' snapped Emerald. 'I hate my harp, and you're as bad as the others—Laver this—Laver that—Laver something else.' She gave an impatient flick of her green tail and disappeared round a large rock.

The Mermaid Mother sighed, and went to the nursery cave where the little ones played safely. She lifted the baby from her cradle and began rocking her and singing to her. Were her children only to be safe and sound when in their own nursery? Would they all grow bigger and want to leave home?

Chapter 22

THE END OF THE PIER

Emerald felt she must do something daring and dashing, and do it now. She did not want to run away and live somewhere else—she remembered Bubbles in his narrow, cramping tank in the zoo, with never a chance to swim or dive and no friendly face to comfort him. Or only Sid and his freckles. No, she wanted an adventure, but an adventure that she would enjoy and that everyone would want to hear about again and again. She would stay away just long enough to give the family a fright, and make them miss her. Then she would come back, all mysterious smiles and secrets, and when they'd begged her to tell them her adventures— well, she *might* give in and tell. But they'd have to beg very hard, very hard indeed.

That night she did not sleep at all, but got up early and started on the long swim to adventure, taking her harp with her. She did not swim towards the sandy bay they all knew, where the land-children played and paddled, but the other way instead, round a rocky headland, where none of the three sea-children had yet been. That would be an adventure to start off with, to explore a new stretch of coast. She turned inland with swift, easy strokes.

When she rounded the headland where the waves broke in foam on the rocks, she saw, as she neared the shore, that it was completely different from Sandy Bay. There was indeed a beach with a border of sand, but beyond it was a white strip of promenade, and beyond that row upon row of white houses with grey slate roofs, climbing up the hillside. The curve of the bay was broken by a pier, jutting out into the sea. Emerald swam towards this pier to have a closer look at it, and as she got nearer she saw that the wooden supports were crusted with seaweed and mussels and barnacles. She liked the fishy, salty, seaweedy smell.

A ladder hung down to the water at the end of the pier, the top of it attached to the white railings.

There was no one about, which Emerald thought was very odd. She had no idea that it was only six o'clock in the morning and that the children and other people staying in the little town were still asleep in their beds. She climbed the ladder and found herself at the end of the pier. There was a gay little building, striped in red, white and blue. She looked inside and saw there were rows and rows of seats, all facing a stage at the far end. Something exciting must happen on this stage and the people in the seats would watch. She was not sure what it could be. Just then she heard footsteps, and saw two men with fishing rods and knapsacks walking along the pier. They were going to fish, with rods and lines and not, like Patrick and Davy, with nets. Emerald looked round quickly for somewhere to hide. She parted the gay curtains that hung in front of the stage and slipped inside. Here she felt safe.

The stage had very little on it, except a piano, a piano

Emerald climbed the ladder and found herself at the end of the pier.

stool, two music stands and a sofa covered in velvet. Behind the stage was another room, and this she found more interesting. Clothes hung from pegs on the wall, some of them very pretty and quite unlike those she had seen other people wear.

There were several dance dresses with frills. One or

two cloaks and a hat with a curling feather. Coloured tights, a crown.

I know, decided Emerald, they are dressing-up clothes. Sometimes Bubbles and Laver and she dressed up in strands of seaweed, with crowns of shells, and made up dances to amuse the little ones, and their parents. These land-people perhaps did the same.

There was a table with a large mirror above it, and on the table was powder, red stuff in pots, wigs and beards and a fine, curly, black moustache. Emerald tried on a fuzzy black wig. She thought she looked almost grown up in it.

There was also a narrow bed with a few cushions strewn over it. Emerald suddenly felt tired after her long swim and her adventures. Also she had come away with no breakfast. She lay on the bed and almost at once fell asleep. Just before she drifted off, she noted several large hampers on the floor with *THE MERRY MAKERS* painted on the labels in bold black letters.

Chapter 23

DISCOVERY

THERE WAS NOTHING to disturb Emerald as the fishermen were some way off and no one else came to the end of the pier. She made up for the previous night when she had hardly slept at all, and she might have slept even longer if the door into the room where she lay had not been opened. Six people came in. She heard voices and wondered, half awake and half asleep, if they were the voices of The Merry Makers.

It was too late to hide anywhere else, so she lay with her eyes closed and hoped no one would notice her.

Some of the voices were men's and some were women's. One complained they would hardly have time to get ready for the afternoon's performance. Another said that very few people would come, as it wasn't raining or windy, and people nowadays had to be drawn into the pavilion by bad weather.

People have no appreciation of art, said someone else. Not if the sun is shining.

Do you blame them? said another voice.

While this conversation was going on, the people were busily getting ready for the afternoon performance. Emerald watched them through her half-closed eyes. Some were making up at the table with the large mirror above, dabbing on rouge and powder, putting on false eyelashes—and one settling a wig on her head. Others were slipping into some of the costumes hanging on the pegs. When the young lady in the yellow wig burrowed into one of the hampers marked THE MERRY MAKERS to find a scarf, she glanced towards the bed and gave a squeal of surprise.

'Look, everyone. A mermaid!'

Everyone looked and exclaimed with amazement.

'Don't look so frightened,' said the golden-haired lady to Emerald. 'We're all madly busy because the show starts at three o'clock. You just lie there and rest. You'll hear quite a bit of it and it may amuse you. We can't explain now or find out how you got here. But we really like having you, don't we, chaps?'

'We sure do,' came from the others.

'Are you The Merry Makers?' asked Emerald timidly.

'We're supposed to be—that's the name of our show. Did you read it on the hamper? You're a clever little mermaid to be able to read.'

'Billy Bones taught me.'

'Well, afterwards, when we're having tea, you can tell us about Billy Bones and how you got here. Gosh, five more minutes.'

The Merry Makers were obviously delighted with their discovery of Emerald and as they passed the bed they all patted her or shook hands with her or stroked her hair. One motherly lady gave her a kiss. She had never had so many people pleased to see her before, and she liked it.

She could hear snatches of the show and thought The

The Merry Makers were very clever entertainers.

Merry Makers were very clever. One played the violin.
Another the piano. Several danced and they all sang.
They could all act, too and they performed short plays
which made the audience laugh. In fact the audience

laughed a great deal. 'The Merry Makers' was a good name.

After a last chorus, in which the audience joined, the show was over and the company gathered round Emerald with mugs of tea, while a bag of buns was passed round. Emerald was supplied with tea and a bun, but made rather slow progress with both. She felt so much at ease with these strange but friendly people that she soon found herself telling them how she had swum away from home to have an adventure of her own.

'You go back,' said Dolly, the motherly one. 'Your poor mum'll be in such a state. Crying her eyes out, I shouldn't wonder.'

'I don't want to go home yet,' said Emerald. 'I like being here so much. I'll go back later when they've had a bit of a fright. Bubbles was away for weeks and weeks and they were delighted to see him again. I want them to be delighted to see me.'

'She could stay with us for a time,' said Mr Punch, who appeared to be the boss. 'She might be able to do a turn. We need new talent. Can you do any of the things you heard us doing this afternoon, little mermaid?'

'Oh no, Mr Punch. I'm not clever like you.'

'Then what's this?' said Luke, removing her harp from behind a cushion. 'Can you play it?'

'Not very well,' said Emerald, hanging her head. 'I don't practise enough.'

'Have a try now, and let's hear you,' said Mr Punch. 'You needn't be afraid of us. We can't play a note on a harp. We wouldn't know how to begin. Play us a tune, love. Anything you like. Even a five-finger exercise, if you have such things in harp music. Come along. Don't be shy.'

Her hands trembling with excitement and terror, Emerald played *Fishes Swim in Water*, the first piece her mother had taught her. The Merry Makers sat in silence without moving, listening to every note. When she had finished they all clapped and smiled.

'Marvellous! Marvellous!' pronounced Mr Punch. 'Will you join us for a week or two? A mermaid will be a great attraction, and a mermaid who plays the harp will bring in crowds. You, Rubens,' he said to a tall dark young man. 'Do a rough-out for a bill now, before the evening show. Put "Mermaid" in large letters at the top and do a sketch of one with a harp. We'll be playing at Newton next week where the hall's three times the size of this little pavilion. We'll fill it to bursting, see if we don't. You practise a few more pieces, Mermaid. They'll cry out for an encore. Why, we've not had a lucky break like this since that girl who could tie herself into knots.'

'What happened to her?' asked Emerald.

'She tied herself in a knot she couldn't undo. Had to go to hospital to be disentangled. Very sad. She was never the same again. Well, will you join us, Mermaid?'

'Yes, I will. And I'll practise hard too. I'll improve. I promise I will.'

So Emerald found herself one of The Merry Makers. She was kept hidden away while they played in the pier pavilion, but she watched and listened and made herself useful in many small ways, sewing on buttons, curling hair and prompting if anyone forgot his or her parts in a play. Everyone called her 'Mermaid' and when she suggested to Mr Punch that her name was really Emerald, he just laughed. 'Mermaid seems to suit you, so Mermaid you'll have to stay,' he said.

At the end of the week, the company, its hampers and luggage and bags and bundles, packed itself into a large red and yellow coach, and they set off for Newton. The journey was not very enjoyable for Emerald, as everyone smoked and she had hardly room to stretch her tail. Looking through the window at the strange sights gave her a headache and she dozed with her head on Dolly's lap. Sometimes Dolly wiped her face with a towel sprinkled with lavender water, or gave her a sip of milk.

Chapter 24

THEY MOVE ON

'LOOK HERE, MERMAID,' said Mr Punch as they approached Newton. 'They're expecting us.'

Emerald sat up and saw bills stuck on walls and fences headed *THE MERRY MAKERS*, and she read in large letters:

'COME AND HEAR THE MUSICAL MERMAID'

Rubens had drawn a beautiful mermaid with golden hair and green tail, a harp in her hand.

'Is that me?' whispered Emerald.

'The spit image,' said Mr Punch heartily.

As they drove through the streets, past shops and houses and occasionally a park, Emerald looked at everything, but did not see what she was looking for.

'Where is the sea, Dolly?' she said at last.

'I don't know exactly, love. Many miles away. Mr Punch, how far is it to the sea?'

'Close on a hundred miles I'd say.'

Tears brimmed Emerald's grey eyes and rolled down her cheeks. 'I thought we were going to another seaside place,' she said huskily. 'I thought we were always to be by the sea. I can't bear it,' and she sobbed in Dolly's comforting arms.

'Of course we can't always be by the sea, Mermaid,' explained Mr Punch. 'We visit theatres and halls inland as well. That little pavilion on the pier where we found you was a very small affair. Now you'll see much grander places with bright lights and velvet curtains and big stages. And sometimes several well-appointed dressing-rooms. Who'd you like to share with?'

'Dolly, please,' said Emerald. But even kind, motherly Dolly had no idea how her heart had sunk. How utterly miserable she felt. No sea! No waves! No beach! No gulls calling! No salt taste in the wind! It was even worse than for Bubbles, who at least had a tank of water to live in. But no, on second thoughts, it was *not* worse than Bubbles' imprisonment, with brutal Mr Bellow and his whip. She was with people she liked very much, and who liked her.

The next night, at the Theatre Royal, she gave her first public performance in a big hall. Again her hands shook, and her cool greenish fingers grew hot and sticky with the stuffy air. But she sat on a little gold chair in the middle of the vast stage and Mr Punch made a speech introducing her as the eighth wonder of the world.

She never saw the sea of eager faces as they merged into a blur. She tried to imagine her Mermaid Mother sitting on a rock, watching and listening and occasionally beating time with a long forefinger with its pearly nail. When she reached the end of *Fishes Swim in Water* the applause was deafening. Every one in the audience clapped, many of them stamped their feet, and others shouted 'Encore'.

Mr Punch had explained to her that 'encore' meant 'play to us again', so when the clapping and stamping

She had to come back again and again to bow and smile.

died down, she bowed and smiled, as she had been taught, and held her harp in the right position. Immediately silence filled the large hall. You could have heard a pin drop.

Feeling less nervous, she played the next piece with steadier fingers. It was called *Treasure Lies in the Ocean.* When she got to the end, the same loud clapping and stamping and shouting broke out again. Mr Punch stood in the wings, hidden from the audience, but he nodded and smiled and made signs for her to play once more.

So she played her last piece, *White Are the Seagulls*, and this time it really was the last one. She left the stage, but had to come back again and again to bow and smile.

After the show, The Merry Makers usually walked back to the house where they were staying, but tonight Mr Punch had ordered a cab as there was a large crowd outside the stage door. Mr Punch and Dolly helped Emerald to find a way through the people, Mr Punch calling out: 'Make way for the little mermaid. Don't push and jostle her. She's fragile and delicate. Don't crowd her like that. She'll not be able to breathe.'

In a few minutes she was safe in the cab, with Dolly's arms round her, and Mr Punch sitting beside the driver. She was tired out when they reached the boarding-house and Dolly put her straight to bed and brought her supper to her.

Chapter 25

FAME

WHEN EMERALD WAS asleep, the other members of the party came round to talk about the evening.

'It was a knock-out!' said Mr Punch. 'The audience went mad. Tomorrow every ticket will be sold and people will be turned away. I've never known anything like it in all my years of show business.'

'She'll have to learn some new pieces,' said Dolly. 'Three aren't enough, and we none of us can play a harp.'

'I know what we could do,' said Jamie, who played the violin. 'She's got a very good musical memory. I'll play an easy catchy tune and I'm sure she'll be able to pick it out on her harp.'

'Now go slow,' said Dolly. 'Don't upset her. She was nervous enough tonight, though it didn't show.'

'Of course I'll go slow,' said Jamie. 'She needn't learn much more music as we move every week. I won't worry her.'

'Mind you don't,' said Mr Punch. 'My little mermaid mustn't be disturbed. She's a little gold mine. That's what she is.'

Jamie was a gentle teacher and Emerald soon knew several more tunes. Every night the hall was full and everybody in the town wanted to see the show because of the mermaid.

Jamie was the Merry Maker who played the violin.

Some disagreeable people complained that it was all a trick and that the mermaid was an ordinary little girl with a fake tail covering her legs. But most people were sure they had seen a real mermaid. And so they had.

The Merry Makers moved on in their red and yellow coach, staying a week here, and a week there, always on the move. Everywhere they performed, the little mermaid was the star turn and though she received the loudest and longest applause each night, nobody was jealous. They were all proud and delighted.

But Emerald was getting tired. She had been away from the sea too long, and even with Dolly's motherly care her tail ceased to glisten and her hair lost its golden sheen. Her little green fingers grew thinner and thinner, even with all the glasses of milk that Dolly persuaded her to drink.

The only thing about her that flourished was her harp playing. Practising every day was what she needed. The Mermaid Mother would have been amazed if she could have heard her little daughter now.

'Next week will set you up,' said Mr Punch, taking her on his knee and feeling how little she weighed. 'Next week we are going to the sea again. We're booked on another pier—this time it's a place called Cockle Bay.'

As the coach neared Cockle Bay, Emerald sat by an open window and took deep breaths of fresh, salt air.

'You look better already,' said Dolly, when the little mermaid ate her third watercress sandwich.

Emerald begged to go for a moonlight swim, but this Mr Punch would not allow.

'You're too precious to risk losing,' he said. 'Far too precious.'

Chapter 26

THE CALL OF THE SEA

BUT THE SOUND of the waves put an idea into Emerald's head that hadn't been there before. She did not speak of it, even to Dolly, though she never forgot it. She had several things to decide first, particularly when the idea was to be tried out. What would be the best time? She must take no risks. She must not fail. She decided to try on the third day.

After the evening performance, The Merry Makers always had a cup of coffee and a snack in the refreshment room on the pier, which stayed open just for them. On the chosen evening, as they sipped their coffee and looked out at the lights shining on the promenade, Emerald took up her harp and played the charm music. The others fell under its spell, one by one. Drinks and snacks were forgotten. They stared in front of them, seeming to see nothing. The lady who served the coffee stood spell-bound behind her counter. Gradually eyes closed. Soon everyone was wrapped in an enchanted sleep, seeing nothing and hearing nothing. They might have been on the moon, their faces appeared so blank and remote.

Emerald gave her six friends a last look. They had been kind and good, and never spoken a cross word. But they must go their way and she must go hers.

She glided through the door, moved to the edge of the

She dived with hardly a splash.

pier, slid between the railings and dived with hardly a splash.

At first she felt strange and scarcely knew where she was or which direction to take. Then she met a porpoise, one of the wisest of creatures, and asked him:

'Which way is the purple seaweed?'

'Come with me. It's where I'm going. There's been a great sorrow in the purple lands. A little mermaid has been lost. We've all been hunting for her for days. I'm returning now to see if she has been found, but I've almost given up hope.' He looked at her intently. 'Can *you* be the missing mermaid?'

'Yes, I am,' whispered Emerald.

'No wonder you look weary, little one. Ride on my back. You weigh no more than a seagull's feather.'

The porpoise rolled swiftly on his way till they found themselves among the purple weed, waving and clinging. Emerald saw the familiar caves and rocks, and a moment later was in her mother's arms. The kind porpoise smiled and rolled away, not waiting to be thanked.

Chapter 27

HOME AT LAST

ALL THE FAMILY welcomed Emerald and kissed her and threw loving green arms round her. But even in her joy and delight, sleep overcame her. She sank on her bed, with Bubbles on one side and Laver on the other.

As for the Mermaid Mother and the Lord of the Sea, sleep was not for them. They watched at the bedside all night long, hand in hand.

'We are together at last,' whispered the Mermaid Mother. 'All of us together.'

'And we'll stay like this always.'

'But when the little ones in the nursery get bigger, supposing they, too, want to go adventuring?'

'Well, we shan't be able to stop them. That's something no one can do. The urge to wander and have adventures is stronger than the ties of home. But home always wins in the end. We've seen that happen three times.'

'I don't think I could bear it if one of the little ones went off to seek freedom. It would be too much.' Tears brimmed the sad grey eyes of the Mermaid Mother.

'They'd learn their lesson in the end,' said the Lord of the Sea. 'Sea-people must stay in the sea, and land-people must live on the land.'

'I hope it will be like that in our family, for ever and

The Mer Family.

ever,' said the Mermaid Mother, drying her tears. 'We must pray to Neptune to keep them safe.'

She looked lovingly at Emerald asleep between her brother and sister. Perhaps her prayer would be heard.